D1452421

JUSTICE FOR MACKENZIE

BADGE OF HONOR: TEXAS HEROES, BOOK 1

SUSAN STOKER

DEDICATION

The Badge of Honor Series is dedicated to every law enforcement officer out there. Every day you put your lives on the line to try to uphold the law and keep the rest of us safe. Every day you may be yelled at, spit on, or shot at. People see you and immediately wonder who you're looking to arrest or get into trouble. But there are also those of us who see you and sigh in relief. Who know you're there to make sure we get home safely, who see the time you spend on the streets and away from your families. So thank you. From the bottom of my heart. Thank you for all you do.

And to the families of law enforcement officers everywhere. You're the strongest men and women I know. You kiss your loved ones as they walk out the door, never knowing what they might be walking into that day on the job. Thank you for letting your loved ones look after us.

You all have my utmost respect. I have taken some creative license with police procedures for the sake of the story, so if I've mangled something in this series that isn't quite right, please know I mean no disrespect to you or to your profession.

CHAPTER 1

DAXTON CHAMBERS barely concealed his impatience with his friend and fellow law enforcement officer, Thomas James "TJ" Rockwell.

"Shut up, TJ. The only reason I agreed to come tonight is because I lost that ridiculous bet."

"Yeah, only *you* were stupid enough to bet the SAFD would win that basketball tournament. You should've gone with the boys in blue rather than those hose jockeys."

"Hey, I've played against some of those guys and they're killers on the court, that's why I thought they'd win. They just had a bad day. Driftwood and Crash played in college, and Squirrel and Taco played in high school. The rest? Doesn't matter, they're usually just there to cause havoc so the others can handle the ball."

TJ laughed. "Yeah, you might be right, but whatever happened, they still lost, so suck it up. This charity thing is only gonna last for a couple of hours. Just be thankful they didn't decide to have a bachelor auction. I think that's been way overdone and is totally cliché, but it's easy and kinda fun in a warped way. But for tonight, we just have to show up, flex our muscles a bit, then leave." TJ ran a hand through his dark, wavy hair.

Dax watched as a tableful of women nearby checked TJ out and then giggled, whispering softly to each other. He chuckled. "Don't look now, but I think you've got an entire table of admirers over there."

Of course TJ looked, but immediately turned back to his friend. "Jesus, Dax. They're barely out of college. No thank you. That time in my life is over. I'm looking for a woman who's serious about a relationship, not a badge bunny who only wants to sleep with as many cops as she can. Been there, done that, got the T-shirt."

"Well, when you find one, hopefully she has a best friend or a sister for me." Dax slapped TJ on the shoulder. "Come on, let's go get a beer and hide out in the corner until this shindig is over. What kind of shifts you got this week? Want to go to that new steak place the guys have been talking about?"

"Let me check and get back to you. They're changing the shifts around and I'm not sure what I'll be doing after next week."

TJ was an officer with the Highway Patrol and Dax was a Texas Ranger. They'd met at a crime scene, and had been friends ever since. Now they were able to collaborate more readily on cases and hang out at law enforcement conferences.

"Are Cruz and Quint coming to this thing tonight?" Dax asked. Cruz Livingston was an FBI agent who worked at the San Antonio Station and Quint Axton was an officer with the San Antonio Police Department.

"Yeah, I think so. Calder, Hayden, and Conor are also supposed to show up. The nonprofit group tried to get law enforcement from all over the city to attend. I haven't seen them in a while and it'll be great to catch up."

Calder Stonewall was one of the medical examiners for San Antonio. Both TJ and Dax had gotten to know him through their cases. Hayden Yates was a sheriff's deputy, the only woman in their tight-knit group, and she'd earned all their respect in a recent rape case. Rape was never easy to investigate or prosecute, and Hayden had worked hard to get justice for the teenager who had been violated by three college men while she'd been attending a party.

The last man in their law enforcement posse was Conor Paxton. He was also probably the person they all knew the least. He worked for the Texas Parks and Wildlife Law Enforcement Division, a member of the SCOUT team that assisted in critical incidents. There were only twenty-five SCOUT members in the entire state of Texas. Conor was quiet and focused, but made a hell of a partner in emergencies.

"Well, we might as well get settled in. There are some speeches first, right? Then the kids are coming out for the talent show?" Dax asked TJ.

"Yeah, our table's off to the side. I asked the organizers not to put us in the middle in case any of us get called away."

"Good thinking."

The men walked around until they found the table with their names on the seating cards. As requested, Cruz, Quint, Calder, Hayden, and Conor had also been assigned seats at the same table.

"As much as I bitched about this tonight, I'm glad I'm here. The kids are always so cute singing and dancing, and it's not often all of us get to be in the same place at the same time, especially when it's for fun and not for work," TJ said after they'd gotten comfortable at the table.

"Agreed," Dax said while nodding.

TJ and Dax settled into their seats and waited for their friends to show up and for the entertainment to start.

* * *

"SANDRA, make sure the kids and their parents know what order everyone is performing. We can't have too much of a break between the acts. We gotta keep this moving." Mackenzie Morgan put her hands on her hips and surveyed the crowd mingling in the large ballroom. This was the second year she'd almost single-handedly organized the annual charity event. It was a rewarding experience, and the law enforcement personnel who showed up were mostly easy on the eyes.

Mackenzie worked for a nonprofit agency called San Antonio Cares (SAC). The company helped all sorts of people in the city, from children to the elderly. They held auctions, charity events, and generally raised money for the less-fortunate people living in the large metropolitan city in Texas. Sandra was the administrative assistant, and one of Mackenzie's biggest helpers for the event. There was no way she'd be able to pull it off without her.

This event was one of their biggest. SAC invited law enforcement officers from all over the city and they usually had a phenomenal turnout. Tonight was no exception. Mackenzie had always liked working with law enforcement. The men and women were almost always very polite and courteous. It was a fallacy that they were all good-looking, though. Mack had seen her share of policemen and women who wouldn't win any beauty contests anytime soon.

However, tonight for some reason, everywhere her gaze landed, she saw almost nothing but good looking officers. Most were in uniform, many wore cowboy hats and boots. Even though the women were also in uniform, Mackenzie was a little jealous of how strong and, yes, beautiful many looked. Mack had always wanted to be svelte and muscular, but she'd been blessed with her mother's genes. She was short, about five feet four, and had too many curves to ever be the type of woman men noticed and fell immediately in lust with.

At a hundred and forty pounds on a good day, Mack was lush. She wasn't embarrassed by her weight or her looks, but with every year that passed without finding someone who she wanted to spend the rest of her life with, she'd begun to worry she never would. At thirty-seven, Mack had dated her fair share of men, and while she'd honestly loved one or two, she'd never felt an all-consuming love; one in which she didn't think she'd be able to live without the other person.

Mackenzie looked around the room once more, her trained eye straining to pick up any problems so she could fix them before they got too big to handle. Her eyes stopped at a table off to the side of the room.

There were two men standing to greet a group of other officers who'd just arrived. They caught her eye because every single person was wearing a slightly different uniform. Usually the men and women tended to clump together in groups of their own kind, for lack of a better word. The SAPD members sat with each other, the FBI agents sat together, and so on. As Mackenzie watched, the six men and one woman sat down after shaking each other's hands and entered into what seemed like a lively conversation.

The man holding a cowboy hat caught Mack's attention and held it. While the other men were all extremely good-looking, Mack made a mental note to suggest to her boss that they revisit the law enforcement calendar for a fundraiser next year. For obvious reasons, this man with the cowboy hat stood out. He had short brown hair. He was tall, but then again, almost every man seemed tall to Mackenzie. She couldn't tell his exact body type, as she was across the room and he was wearing a long-sleeve uniform, but she liked the way he looked people in the eyes as he greeted them, making sure each person knew he was paying attention to them.

Hell, Mackenzie had no idea what drew her eyes to the man, especially since there were handsome men all around her. But there was an attraction, and it was instant and baffling at the same time. She'd never felt a zing like the one she felt looking at this man.

A shout drew her attention past the table to one of the little girls who was supposed to be performing later on. She was shouting at one of her friends as she ran, not paying attention to what was going on around her. A waiter carrying a tray full of empty beer bottles and glasses was right in her path.

Mackenzie immediately started across the room, knowing she wouldn't be able to prevent the accident, but hoping she'd be able to keep the little girl from being hurt.

The little girl crashed into the waiter just as Mackenzie reached them. Performing what had to be an award-winning snatch-and-grab, Mackenzie caught the little girl around the waist just as she bounced off of the waiter's legs.

Mack watched as he teetered and then lurched to the side, trying to avoid dropping the tray on the little girl's head. Inevitably, the tray slid, unbalanced by his sudden movement, and all the glasses fell to the floor in a loud, very noticeable crash.

Mack took a few steps away from the mess on the floor and kneeled down to speak to the child, wanting to make sure she'd gotten there in time to keep her from getting cut by the glass.

"Are you all right?" Mackenzie looked at the nametag attached to the startled girl's sparkly dress. "Cindy? Did the glass hurt you?"

Cindy sniffed and shook her head, putting her thumb in her mouth and sucking hard.

Mackenzie looked up to see a woman striding toward them, and Cindy reached up for her as she got close.

"I'm so sorry, Ms. Morgan," Cindy's mom said as she comforted her daughter.

Seeing Cindy's mom relieved Mackenzie. She liked kids, but wasn't very good with them. "It's okay; I'm just glad Cindy's not hurt. Go ahead and take her to where the other kids are getting ready, I'll take care of this and we'll start the show in a bit. All right?"

"Sure. And thanks. I've never seen someone move so fast before."

Mackenzie nodded absently, already turning back to the waiter. Relieved, she saw two of the caterers there, already cleaning up the mess.

"Are you all right, miss?"

Startled, Mackenzie looked up—right into the eyes of the man she'd been admiring earlier.

Wow. He was even better-looking up close. She briefly noticed the Texas Ranger star on his chest and nodded her head in answer to his question. Damn, Rangers were the best of the best in the state. They had a great reputation and she knew he was way out of her league. Besides, as much as she might want to, she didn't have time to chitchat.

"Yeah, I'm good. It's inevitable that something like this happens with this many people around. You're okay too, yeah? Was anyone hit by the glass? Crap, I gotta make sure they put up a 'wet floor' sign, I don't want anyone slipping. Just what I need, to have a cop slip and hit his head. I'd probably get sued or something. That would be bad karma for sure. Anyway, yeah, I'm good, I gotta get going. Got a shit-ton of stuff to do. Glad you're okay too."

Mackenzie shifted away from the Ranger, knowing she was babbling but not able to stop. She had a tendency to go on and on, especially when she was nervous. She moved away from the man with a pang of regret. She wasn't being coy, she really *didn't* have time to talk to him. She had a show to get started and a mess to make sure was cleaned up.

Dax watched as the brunette walked away from him and over to a woman in black pants and white shirt, who looked as though she worked for the catering company. He smiled, not taking his eyes from the curvy woman's backside. She'd adorably talked on and on, not quite looking him in the eye. It was a refreshing change from the women he encountered on a daily basis. They either flirted shamelessly with him solely based on his looks and the fact he was a Ranger, or they were shifty and elusive, lying their asses off to get out of whatever crime they'd committed.

"Come on, Dax. Get your ass back over here. Calder wants to know what the hell you were thinking, siding with the firefighters over the officers last week," Cruz yelled from the table.

Dax took one last look at the woman, now talking with the lady from the catering company, and sighed. He didn't know her, and had really only said a couple of words to her, but she was cute babbling on with him. Not only that, she had the kind of body he was most attracted to. But he'd had issues in the past with women not wanting to put up with his crazy schedule, and figured with his luck, this woman would probably not be any different.

He turned and headed back to the large table with a deep breath. It would be a long night, taking the good-natured ribbing from his friends. He wouldn't change it for the world.

CHAPTER 2

DAX LOOKED across the police vehicle at TJ. He'd never forget when he met the Highway Patrolman for the first time. TJ had called in the Rangers when the report of a dead body had been made off one of the many rural highways that snaked around San Antonio. Dax met TJ at the scene and they'd immediately clicked. After a long investigation, the men had become friends.

At the moment, TJ was technically off duty, although they were in his official vehicle and they were driving to a steak place that had just opened and had gotten rave reviews. They'd finally synched their schedules and were headed for dinner.

"How's that serial case you've been working on?"

Dax sighed. They'd talked about it for a bit at the charity talent show they'd attended a couple of weeks ago, but it'd gotten worse since then. "Sucks. This guy is good."

"How many bodies have been found so far?"

"Five. All buried alive and called in. Who knows how many more there are, because it's not like we'd ever find the bodies if the bastard didn't let us know where they were."

"What does Calder say about cause of death?"

As one of the medical examiners for Bexar County, Calder was responsible for figuring out the cause of death for all persons who died suddenly, unexpectedly, or violently.

"Asphyxiation, of course. The bastard buries them alive and Calder estimates they stay alive for anywhere from two to ten hours. Fucking torture."

TJ didn't have much to say. It was inevitable that their talk turned to work whenever they got together. Both men were committed to their jobs and getting bad guys off the streets, one way or another.

Just as Dax was about to try to change the subject to something a little less depressing, a blue Honda Civic going the opposite direction flew by them. TJ flipped on the rear-facing radar just in time to clock the car going eighty miles an hour in a sixty zone.

"Hang on."

Dax held on and didn't bother to protest as TJ

slowed just enough to make a safe U-turn and then stepped on the gas to catch up to the speeding car. While technically off duty, every law enforcement officer knew they were never *really* off duty. Someone going that fast could easily kill someone, and it was TJ's duty as an officer to stop them.

Dax grinned as they quickly made up the distance between them and the car. Dax didn't get to work patrol anymore, so it was adrenaline-inducing to be involved in a high speed chase once again. The Honda was no match for the Crown Victoria with its powerful engine, and TJ quickly caught up. He flicked on the police lights while simultaneously radioing the license plate to dispatch. The driver in the car immediately pulled over to the side of the road after seeing the flashing lights in her rear-view mirror.

"Thought you were off duty, TJ," the dispatcher on the other end of the radio said with laughter in her voice.

"Yeah, well, you know how it is."

Dax and TJ pulled over to the shoulder behind the vehicle waiting for dispatch to get back with the vehicle information. They didn't have to wait long.

"Blue, 2011 Honda Civic. Registered to a Mackenzie Morgan, age thirty-seven. Five feet four, one hundred-forty pounds. San Antonio resident. No priors, no record."

"Ten-Four. Thanks." TJ told the dispatcher he'd be out on the traffic stop and put down the mic.

"Sorry, Dax. I'd love to let her off with a warning to speed this up, but I'll have to play it by ear. I'll try to keep it short so we can be on our way. I'm starved. Be right back."

Dax watched as TJ eased out of his patrol vehicle and carefully made his way to the driver's door. The most dangerous part of any traffic stop was making the initial contact with the occupants in a vehicle. There was no way to know if the person or people in the car had weapons and if they would open fire on an officer as he or she came up to the car.

Dax could see the woman in the car holding on to the steering wheel with both hands, as she'd probably been taught.

TJ stood a foot or so away from the door and leaned over a bit, talking to the woman. Dax watched as she reached over to the glovebox and handed some papers out the window to TJ, most likely her license and registration.

Dax couldn't see much of the woman from his vantage point in the front seat of TJ's cruiser, but he could imagine how she looked from the description relayed by the dispatcher. Short and probably curvaceous. Just his type. Oh, Dax had dated all shapes and sizes of women, but he always came back to what he liked best. At an inch over six feet, Dax liked the feeling of being taller and bigger than the woman he was dating. He liked it when she fit into the bend of his arm. Dax hated when a woman was skin and bones. There was nothing like being able to have some flesh to hold on to while pounding in and out of her body.

Dax shifted in his seat. Jesus, he had to get ahold of himself. He was too old to get an erection imagining what the anonymous woman might look like. It'd obviously been way too long since he'd gotten laid. He'd have to see what he could do about that.

TJ turned and came back to the vehicle after a lengthy conversation with the woman in the car. He sat back down and pulled the laptop mounted in the center console to him. He quickly punched in the information from the driver's license in his hand.

"So?" Dax asked, "What was her sob story?"

TJ grinned. "You wouldn't believe it. She was actually really cute."

"Cute?"

"Yeah, she started babbling like I don't think I've heard anyone do before. She wasn't really trying to get out of the ticket, and she wasn't trying to excuse herself...she was just spilling her guts."

Dax tilted his head. What did TJ's words remind him of?

"She babbled about how she'd had a terrible day at work with her boss from hell. Then she explained she had to go home and be tortured by her family for being single and childless. *Then* she went into the cutest fucking rant about how she hated when people would zoom by her on the highway and not even care they were going so fast. Somehow she then changed the topic and began to talk about eighteen-wheelers on the roads before I cut her off."

"What was her name again?" Dax asked, the niggling feeling even stronger. He still couldn't figure out why he had it though.

"Mackenzie Morgan. She's clean. She's never even had a parking ticket before, at least not here in San Antonio. I'm going to let her off with a warning."

"A warning? That's not like you. You must've *really* thought she was cute."

Laughing, TJ handed over the driver's license to Dax while saying, "Yeah, she's cute, but that's not why I'm letting her off. She was honestly mortified she'd been going so fast."

"Suuuure that's the reason." Dax laughed then looked down at the license he held in his hand.

Surprisingly, the picture actually wasn't as horrible as most tended to be.

Mackenzie A. Morgan. Just as the dispatcher said, she was nine inches shorter than he was. She had brown hair in the photo and was smiling crookedly. Dax had the thought that even her eyes were smiling. Why did she look so familiar to him?

TJ just shook his head at Dax and held out his hand for her license. After Dax handed it over, TJ got out of the car. Before going back to the Honda, he said, "Besides, it's just too much trouble to write up the ticket. We have reservations."

Dax laughed out loud as TJ headed back to tell Mackenzie the good news. TJ had always been a sucker for a pretty face, and Ms. Morgan was certainly one of those.

TJ was gone a bit too long to deliver a simple warning to the woman, and Dax frowned, not liking the feeling in his gut.

Fuck, it was jealousy. He was jealous of his damn friend. It looked as if they were in another in-depth conversation and Dax saw the woman shaking her head several times. His leg bounced up and down with impatience. How could he be jealous of his friend? Fuck, it was just a traffic stop, one of thousands TJ had made over his career. It wasn't as if he was arranging a date with the woman...was he?

Dax himself had pulled over his share of people before he became a Ranger, so why was this one different? Dax didn't want to admit it, but it was because of the woman behind the wheel. He hadn't seen her face in person, just the image on her driver's license, but he still had a feeling he knew her. His gut was screaming at him, but he didn't know why.

TJ finally nodded at the woman and came back to the patrol car. He sat down and pulled the laptop over to him to close out the traffic stop. Dax watched as the Honda pulled sedately away from the side of the road and continued on until it was out of sight. Feeling as if he'd somehow lost something important, and that he should've at least gotten out and met the woman—even if that would've been highly unusual—Dax frowned. It was too late now.

"What was that about?"

"Damn. Did I say she was cute before? Because she was even more adorable the second time. I told her she was off the hook and gave her the warning and she broke into another long soliloquy about how relieved she was and how I'd protected her clean record."

"So she was flirting with you?" Dax asked sharply.

TJ looked over at his friend. "That's not how it was."

"Then how was it?"

"Look, I don't pick up women I pull over, Dax, Jesus. Besides, she's not my type. She just started babbling again about how thankful she was. Oh, she also mentioned she'd just helped with the same charity event we were at the other week. She told me she always knew cops weren't the hardasses we tried to portray and she thanked me for all the money her group raised that night."

"Holy shit, that's it!" Dax exclaimed.

"What's it?" TJ asked, his face scrunched up in confusion.

"That's where I recognized her from. I saw her that night, at the charity thing. Remember when the waiter dropped the tray?"

"Vaguely."

"She was the one who came over to help."

"And? I don't get your point, Dax."

Dax remembered how the woman had babbled on and on with him before abruptly turning away to take care of business. He smiled. "Can I have her number?"

TJ looked at his friend in disbelief. "What?"

"Her number. I know it's in the computer. Give it to me."

"You can't call her out of the blue and ask her out, Dax."

"Why not?"

"She's gonna think you're a stalker."

"No, she won't."

"Besides, it's against the law for me to give it to you, and you know it."

Dax tried to smile at his friend charmingly. "Come on, man. Please? I never got her name at the thing the other week, but I think it's fate that you pulled her over tonight. I had no way of finding her before, but now I do."

"You have it bad."

Dax just kept smiling.

"Oh all right, but if I get in trouble, I'm siccing the review board on your ass."

"Cool."

"Jesus, I feel like a dating service. She really got to you, huh?"

"Yeah. There's just something about her. I'm not sending out wedding invitations. Hell, I'm not even saying I want to date her. But I'm interested enough to call her up and see if anything comes out of it."

TJ started the car and, after looking both ways to make sure no cars were coming, did a U-turn in the road and headed back the way they were going before pulling Mackenzie over.

"Ready for food?" TJ was obviously trying to change the subject.

"Oh, hell yeah. Think you can avoid pulling anyone else over in the next thirty minutes so we can actually get something to eat?"

"Funny guy."

Dax smiled. He loved being part of the brotherhood of law enforcement. It didn't matter that he was a Texas Ranger and TJ was a Highway Patrol officer. Law enforcement was law enforcement and they all worked together on cases. Neither he nor TJ had ever been married, and they liked it that way. Dax knew it was tough to be married to a cop and he hadn't been able to find a woman who could handle it yet. At forty-six years old, he figured he never would. He mentally shrugged. He didn't care. He had his career and his friends. Life was good.

But for the first time in a really long time, he was excited about the prospect of a date. He hadn't lied to TJ. There was something about Ms. Mackenzie Morgan that got to him. He hoped he could find out what it was and either get it out of his system, or see where it could lead.

"Pedal to the metal then. Let's go eat."

CHAPTER 3

MACKENZIE SIGHED HEAVILY as she made her way up to her apartment. Getting pulled over was the icing on the cake to a very long, craptastic day. She couldn't believe she'd been so lost in her head she'd been going twenty miles over the speed limit. Thank God the officer decided to give her a warning instead of a ticket.

After opening the door, Mackenzie slipped her keys back into her purse and dumped it on the small table in the entryway. She shut and locked the door, then hung her coat on the hook on the wall in the small hallway.

She then kicked off her shoes and padded down the hall to her living room. Mackenzie collapsed on her sofa, put her head back, and closed her eyes. Damn, she was glad to be home.

The day had started out all right. Mackenzie had arrived at work with plenty of time to spare and settled into her chair at her desk. She'd had a lot of paperwork to reconcile after the charity event, even weeks later, and had been well into it when her horrible boss had called her into her office.

Nancy Wood was one of a kind. She was around four inches taller than Mackenzie, but was about thirty pounds lighter. She was scary skinny. Not only that, but her hair was long and black, like down-to-her-butt long. It swished around her as she walked because she refused to wear it up or braid it. With her hair, her pointed nose, and long face, Nancy was an odd looking woman. She never smiled and loved ordering everyone in the office around. Everyone made fun of her behind her back and called her the "wicked witch of the SAC."

The woman thought she was much more important than she really was. Nancy had spent two hours going over the spreadsheets of the donations they'd received and the money that had been spent. It drove Mack crazy because ultimately the finances were her responsibility. She hated having her boss double-check her work as if she was a fifth grader.

Not long after she'd finally gotten out of the meeting with her boss, the phone rang. It was her mom wanting to invite her over for an impromptu family dinner.

Mackenzie loved her mom and her brothers, but they simply didn't understand her. First they'd started on her choice to live in an apartment instead of buying a house. She knew at her age she should have probably bit the bullet and invested in a property by now, but she liked living in an apartment. She liked being able to call the manager when something went wrong and not have to deal with it herself. She wasn't very handy, so it was nice that she could put the responsibility for fixing whatever was wrong on someone else. Mackenzie was also especially grateful she didn't have to worry about any kind of yard work.

Nevertheless, every time she got together with her family—every single time—they harped on her for being thirty-seven and unmarried. It wasn't that Mackenzie didn't want to be married; she just hadn't found someone who she wanted to spend the rest of her life with.

She sighed. Mackenzie knew she was picky. It wasn't a secret. Every time she thought she'd found the perfect guy, he'd do something or say something to make her reconsider. Then she'd grab hold of that one little thing and eventually it would grow bigger and bigger and she'd become more and more discontent and the relationship would end. Mackenzie's best friend, Laine, told her all the time she was like Seinfeld, finding stupid reasons to dump men. Most of the time her relationships would end with the man throwing up his hands in disgust and walking out the door.

Mackenzie wasn't an idiot; she knew it was her fault for nitpicking the men she dated to death and making them not want to stay, but she had no idea how to stop. And if a little voice inside her wanted the man to stay despite her being a bitch, she'd never admit it.

She had some bad habits, she knew it, but she didn't think they were horrible enough for a guy to break up with her over them. One boyfriend told her he thought her habit of rambling on and on was cute, but toward the end of their relationship, he'd admitted it was embarrassing for him when she said whatever she was thinking around others with no filter, and that if she ever wanted to keep a man, she'd better rein that in. Jerk.

She recalled the conversation she'd had tonight with her brothers. They'd been unusually blunt with her, and their words had struck home all the more because Mackenzie knew they were right on most counts.

"Mack, what do you expect a guy to do when

you're going at him every day for stupid shit? Take it? No way."

"But Mark, if he loved me, he'd see how upset I am and change."

"I love you, sis, but no. First of all, I've heard you complain about how the men you date want you to change some of the things you do, so I don't see how you can stand there and say that if someone loved you, they wouldn't ask *you* to change, but you can turn around and bitch that *he's* not doing things the way you think he should. You can't expect a guy to alter the way he does the dishes, for Christ's sake, just because you want him to put the plates in the dishwasher one way and he does it another. It's ridiculous. You're *looking* for ways to push them away and you harp on them over and over until they decide you're just not worth it."

Mackenzie lowered her head. She knew Mark was right. Then Matthew had started in on her.

"Seriously, I've seen the way you are with them. Remember that one Thanksgiving when we all had to sit around and listen to you bicker with…whatever his name was? It was crazy. You wouldn't let anything go. Hell, the man couldn't even sit and watch football without you telling him he was doing it wrong."

Mackenzie's mom joined in as well. "All we're saying, sweetie, is lighten up. You'll never find a guy who's perfect. You just have to learn to give a little more when you're in a relationship."

Mackenzie sighed and grabbed the pillow next to her on the couch, held it to her stomach, and buried her face in it. She was such a headcase. She didn't know why she was this way…strike that, she did, but she hated to admit it to herself, or anyone else. Her first real adult boyfriend had done the exact same thing to *her*, nitpicked everything she'd done, and apparently, she'd committed everything he'd done to memory and decided it was how relationships were supposed to work. It was a self-fulfilling prophesy apparently, because every man she'd dated since that first man, she'd done the same thing to. Nitpicked stupid little things he did, until he got fed up and left.

Mackenzie knew it was stupid, knew *she* was being stupid. Her brother was right, it didn't really matter if a man left his shoes in the closet, or on the bathroom floor. But now that she was used to doing things the way *she* thought they should be done, it was hard to stop. Hell, her mom had told her often enough that she'd been an extremely stubborn child, now she was a stubborn adult.

But she was a romantic. Always had been. As a kid, she'd made her mom buy her every Disney movie and she'd watched them over and over. *Cinderella, Snow White*...it didn't matter. As long as the fairy princess ended up with the prince, Mackenzie had loved it. It'd probably skewed her thinking.

Mackenzie turned her mind from her family—as well-meaning as they were, they still depressed her —and back to the incident on her way home.

She'd been horrified when she'd been pulled over. Mackenzie was a good girl, never had even a parking ticket before, so being pulled over was not a fun experience. She'd been speeding because she wanted nothing more than to get home and into some comfy clothes and relax.

The police officer had actually been very nice, all things considered. He'd taken her license and registration and she'd felt humiliated waiting for him to come back and give her a ticket. Of course she'd babbled on and on to him. She even saw him laughing with the man who'd been in the car with him.

Mackenzie had glanced into her rear-view mirror and watched as the officer and whoever the man was sitting next to him laughed with each other. She'd felt the blush rise on her face, hoping they weren't laughing at her. But the other man was definitely good-looking. Mackenzie had always had a thing about men in uniform. There was just something about seeing a crisp shirt, a pressed pair of pants, a badge, and all the accoutrements that came with whatever the man's profession was, that pushed her buttons.

She had no idea how tall the man in the passenger seat was, but he had dark hair and a nice smile. Mackenzie shook her head. Sad that that was all it took to get her interested.

Suddenly Mack sat up straight on the sofa and said out loud to her empty apartment, "Holy shit!"

The man in the car had been the Ranger she'd lusted after at the charity event!

At least she thought it was the same man. She couldn't be sure, but she remembered how she'd talked about the event the other night with the officer outside her car and he'd mentioned he'd been there. If he was there, the man sitting next to him in his car most likely was too. It probably really *was* the man she'd briefly spoken to at the charity event.

She buried her face in her hands. How freaking humiliating. Great. Just great. This was all she needed on top of everything else that had happened today. Mackenzie had spilled her entire lunch in her lap when she'd misjudged the table and put her plate down too close to the edge. She'd always been a klutz and was constantly spilling and breaking things, as well as tripping over her own feet.

All in all, it'd been a shitty day and she hadn't been able to stop the tears from falling while she'd waited for the officer to come back with the ticket she knew she deserved. He'd been very nice to her. Mackenzie didn't have any excuses for speeding; she'd just wanted to get home and wasn't watching how fast she was driving.

Getting a warning instead of a ticket had been one of the only good things about the day. Mackenzie took a deep breath. Thank goodness today was finally over. She got up off her couch and headed into her bedroom, not bothering to check the mail she'd picked up.

She stripped off her shirt, threw it into the laundry hamper and took off her bra, just dropping it on the floor where she stood. Her pants came next, along with her panties. Mackenzie walked naked into her bathroom, where she got ready for bed. It was early, but she didn't care.

Mackenzie had always preferred to sleep naked. She had expensive fifteen hundred thread count sheets that felt smooth and silky next to her body. Mackenzie once had a boyfriend who chided her for her penchant to sleep without anything on, telling her she didn't have the type of body that looked good naked and she'd be sexier if she covered it up with a nightie. She'd dumped his ass the next day. Fuck him.

Mackenzie knew she wasn't beautiful, and that was okay. She wasn't a troll, she had great legs, but she was too short to ever be considered classically pretty. She liked to eat, she liked her sweets and loved pasta and hated to work out as well. She'd never be stick thin, and that was perfectly all right with her. Rather than wishing to be thin, Mackenzie always wished to be taller instead. It was tiring always looking at people's chests or necks instead of being able to look them in the eye. Not to mention the way men would try to look down any shirt she wore. Jerks. Mackenzie had also hated wearing heels, she was way too clumsy to pull off a sophisticated look in them, so she was stuck at her five feet four.

She climbed into her queen-size bed and under her comforter and fleece blanket and snuggled in for the night. Mackenzie didn't bother picking up her e-reader to finish the romance she'd been reading. She wasn't in the mood to read about how some lucky woman got her happy ever after with a hunk of a man...even if it was only fiction.

She closed her eyes, trying not to relive the day, and surprisingly fell asleep quickly. She dreamed of a dark-haired policeman backing her against a police car and leaning down to kiss her.

CHAPTER 4

AFTER WHAT SEEMED like the longest week in the history of her life, Mackenzie sat on her couch with a cup of double-dark hot chocolate, watching one of her favorite movies of all time, *Ever After*. The acting wasn't the best, and the accents were horrendous, but since it was a version of *Cinderella*, Mackenzie loved it.

Laine was supposed to have come over to watch movies with her, but she had a date. Mackenzie and Laine had made a deal a long time ago that if they had plans and one of them got asked out, they'd go on the date, with no hard feelings. Of course, they'd made the pact when they were in middle school, and certainly didn't have to honor it all these years later, but since they were both still hoping their prince was out there, the pact was still in force today.

Mackenzie's cell phone rang, startling her, and when she jerked, of course the drink she'd been holding spilled all over herself. Cursing and wiping the hot drink off her pants, Mackenzie reached over and swiped the small screen to answer the phone without looking at the number, figuring it was Laine calling to dish about her date.

"Hello?"

"Hello. Is this Mackenzie Morgan?"

"Yeah, who is this?"

"My name is Daxton Chambers. I'm a Texas Ranger and was calling to follow up with you after your traffic infraction earlier this week."

Mackenzie's blood ran cold. *Oh my God. Was she in trouble? Was she supposed to get a ticket after all? Was she not supposed to drive away when she did? She didn't know the protocol when you'd been given a warning...Wait, she was given a warning, wasn't she? Fuck.*

She did what she usually did when she was nervous, she talked—fast. "I'm so sorry. Was I not supposed to leave when I did? I thought it was a warning. I didn't mean to break any laws. Shit. Do I have to turn myself in somewhere or something? I really didn't mean to be speeding, I'd had a horrible day, and that was just the icing on the cake. Seriously, Officer, I swear I'm not like that usually."

"Ma'am—"

Mackenzie kept talking. "I didn't think there was a fine with a warning, but I admit I didn't really look at the paper that closely. I was too relieved I didn't get an actual ticket and I just stuffed it into my bag and forgot about it. I'd look at it now, but it was in my purse and my stupid nail polish busted open inside my purse and it got all over it and I had to throw it away. Hell, I had to throw away the whole purse because the lining was completely ruined, but I swear—"

"Ma'am." The Ranger's voice was stronger now.

"Seriously, it was my own fault. I don't know why I had the stupid nail polish in there in the first place. I'm extremely clumsy and I thought I'd bring it with me and do my nails at lunch, which is stupid, because my nails just break anyway, the polish wouldn't really do any good, but I thought that maybe I'd make the effort because my mom and brothers have been on me to try harder with my appearance—"

"Mackenzie, shush for a second."

Mackenzie closed her eyes, mortified. Jesus. She'd been going on and on, but she was so nervous. This guy must think she was a complete idiot. "Sorry," she whispered, waiting to hear what he wanted.

Mackenzie waited, but the line was silent. She felt sick. "Hello?"

"I just wanted to make sure you were really going to be quiet and let me talk." His voice was low, rumbly, and full of humor.

"Um..."

He continued, and Mackenzie could tell he was completely amused with her. At least he was amused and not pissed.

"You're not in trouble, and it *was* just a warning. I was there that night when Officer Rockwell pulled you over. I don't know if you remember me, but I met you briefly at the charity event a couple of weeks ago. I just wanted to check in with you and make sure you were all right after getting pulled over."

Mackenzie was stunned into silence, and that was highly unusual for her. Was this really the guy she'd met and lusted over? It couldn't be. There was no way he wanted to check to make sure she was all right. Something else had to be going on. "You wanted to check to make sure I was all right?" She couldn't help the question.

"Yeah."

"Uh, why?"

"Because I was worried about you."

"You were worried about me."

The man chuckled on the other end of the line. "You gonna repeat everything I say, Mackenzie?

Yeah, I was worried about you, but more than that, I wanted to call because I remembered you from the charity event."

Mackenzie didn't really know what to say. This was just so odd. "You said you were a Texas Ranger? You're not a Highway Patrol officer, right? Why were you there, too?"

"Officer Rockwell and I were on our way to dinner when you zipped by. We made the stop, then continued on to the restaurant."

"Oh my God," Mackenzie whispered, disconcerted. "He was off duty and had to stop me? And, you were on the way to dinner?"

Dax was enjoying the hell out of his conversation with Mackenzie. She was incredibly entertaining and just as interesting as she was that night he'd met her. Besides that, he'd never had a conversation like this with a woman before. She zipped from one topic to another without seeming to breathe. "Yeah, I was there."

"Okay, that's it. I'm never driving again. I'm going to throw my license away and become a hermit who never leaves my house."

Dax chuckled. "I don't think I'd go that far. But you want to answer my original question now? Everything okay?"

Mackenzie huffed out a breath and leaned back

against the couch, one hand holding the phone to her ear and the other still holding the cup of cocoa in her hand. "I'm fine."

"You're fine." His words weren't stated as a question, but Mackenzie could tell they were a question nevertheless.

"What was your name again?"

"Daxton Chambers."

"Well, Daxton Chambers, I don't know if you are really who you say you are, but I'm going to give you the benefit of the doubt here. If you must know, I'd had a really crappy day when I was pulled over. I know, everyone has crappy days, but that was a *really* crappy day. To top off a crappy day at work, where I spilled my lunch and didn't have any chance to get anything to eat to replace it, and where I got yelled at by my horrible boss for something stupid, I had just spent two hours at my mom's house where I was told I was basically a dried-up old maid and it was all my fault because I'm too picky and I chase every guy away. So yeah, when I got pulled over, I can't say I was in a happy place. But the day ended with a warning instead of a ticket, so my felon-free life is still squeaky clean and I've moved on."

Mackenzie forced herself to stop talking. She was such a dork.

"In case you're wondering, I'm not easily chased

away."

"Shit!" At his surprising words, Mackenzie had spilled her mug of hot chocolate—again—and it was now seeping into the cushions of her couch as well as dripping off onto the floor. "Shit. Shit. Shit! Hang on. Fuck." Mackenzie threw the phone down and frantically looked around for something to mop up the drink. Seeing nothing, she sighed and whipped off the T-shirt she was wearing. It was already stained with who-the-hell-knew-what, so she might as well use it as a towel. She held it to the couch, trying to clean up the bulk of the mess. She kneeled on the floor and tried to mop up the liquid on the couch as well as what was dripping over the side.

Mackenzie reached over with her free hand and brought her phone back up to her ear. "Hello? Are you still there?"

"What happened? Are you hurt?" Dax's voice was hard and urgent.

"Sorry! No, I'm fine. I spilled my drink. That's all. I told you I was clumsy."

Dax relaxed back against the counter where he'd been standing. For a second, he was afraid Mackenzie had been hurt and he'd have to call 911 for her. He grinned. "I gotta say, this has to be one of the most fascinating phone calls I've ever had with a woman."

41

"Oh Lord." Mackenzie rested her head on the cushion in front of her. The couch muffled her voice when she mumbled, "I'm seriously never leaving the house again."

"I hope that's not true, since I'm coming over tomorrow night to pick you up and take you to dinner."

Dax waited for a response, but didn't get one. He knew Mackenzie hadn't hung up because he could still hear her breathing on the other end of the phone. He hadn't been this interested in a woman since…well, in a really long time. Mackenzie was cute as hell and he knew she wasn't even trying to be. That was what drew him in the most.

"Mackenzie? You still there?"

"Yeah, but I think I'm having hallucinations. Maybe the cocoa was bad or something."

"You're not hallucinating and I don't think hot chocolate *goes* bad. I'm coming over tomorrow night. I'll be there around six to take you out to dinner. It'll be casual, so don't wear anything fancy."

"I don't think I own anything fancy. I'd just ruin it anyway; I'd probably drop my fork in my lap or something and mess it up."

Dax noticed Mackenzie hadn't tried to get out of the date. He smiled again. "Good. You gonna be there tomorrow at six when I get there?"

"I don't think this is how it works."

"How what works?"

"I don't think you can just tell me you're coming to get me and you're taking me out to eat."

"Why not?"

"Why not what?"

"Why isn't it how it works?

"I don't know you."

"I'm trying to change that."

Mackenzie tried to get the conversation back on track. "How do you know where I live?"

"Mack, I'm a Ranger. I was in the car when TJ stopped you and ran your information. I know where you live."

"Are you really a Texas Ranger?"

"Yeah."

"Are you gonna kidnap and kill me like that psycho has been doing to women around here?"

"No."

"This is weird."

"It's not weird," Dax put every ounce of sincerity in his voice that he could. "I met you a few weeks ago and thought you were cute. Hell, I haven't met anyone like you in a long, long time. I watched you walk away from me with regret. I didn't know your name. I didn't know anything about you, but I liked what I saw and what I heard, anyway. Then it was as if fate took hold, because there you were…again. What are the odds you'd be on the road you were, speeding, and I'd be on that same road? I'd like to take you out to dinner and get to know you more. Maybe we won't get along. Maybe we'll go out once and decide, mutually, that we should be friends, or not at all. Give me a chance, Mackenzie. I'll be there tomorrow night at six. Will you be there?"

"I'll be here."

Every muscle in Dax's body relaxed. He hadn't realized how tightly he was holding himself until after Mackenzie had accepted his date. He hadn't planned on asking her out, but there was no way he could sit there and listen to how incredibly adorable she was, rambling on about nail polish and how clumsy she was and *not* ask her out. TJ was going to give him a rash of shit, but Dax didn't care. For the first time in a long time, he was looking forward to a date.

Most of the time women hit on *him*, simply because of the uniform he wore. It was nice, for once, to be the pursuer instead of the pursued. Mack wasn't going to know what hit her.

"Good." Dax lowered his voice. "I'm looking forward to it."

"But, seriously, don't get your hopes up, Daxton. I don't do one-night stands."

"I don't recall asking you to sleep with me."

Mackenzie buried her head even farther into the couch cushion, embarrassed. "Shit. See? I'm totally awkward and shouldn't really be out with actual people in public. I should be locked away so people can point and laugh at what an honest-to-God dork looks like. What I meant was that I'm not good at relationships. Seriously. You know how old I am, you know my height and weight...I told you what my own family thinks...I'm just...me."

"And I like 'just' you, Mackenzie. At least what I've seen and heard so far. We'll go out and see what happens. I promise I won't propose tomorrow if you won't jump my bones in the parking lot. Deal?"

Mackenzie laughed out loud. "I think I can agree to that."

"Great. Then I'll see you tomorrow at six."

"Okay, Daxton. See you then."

"Bye."

"Bye."

Mackenzie clicked off her phone and sat up on her haunches in front of her couch for a moment before leaning over and stuffing her face into one of the cushions and screaming at the top of her lungs.

She sat up with a smile on her face. A date. A real live date. Wow. She couldn't wait to talk to Laine.

CHAPTER 5

THE NEXT AFTERNOON, Dax met TJ for lunch. They were sitting in a local diner that had amazingly good food for a place that looked like a broken-down building.

"You did it? Shit, Dax. I thought you were just messing with me," TJ said incredulously.

"Well, I wasn't. And yes, I did call her. I checked, she said she was fine, then I asked her out."

TJ shook his head and finally smiled at his friend, slyly, testing him. "And if I wanted in there?"

Dax didn't even flinch. "Too late my friend. You snooze, you lose. You should've said something when I asked you for her number. You knew I was gonna call her."

TJ threw his head back and laughed, then shook

his head at Dax. "You're crazy. Asking out a woman you don't even know."

Dax got serious. "I'd changed my mind since we talked that night. I knew it was crazy to ask her out. Seriously. I was just gonna call her up and make sure she was okay, but then she opened her mouth. She was rambling on and on about nail polish and being so…real…that I couldn't resist. You know how it is, most women try to act serious and proper around us when they think they're in trouble, then flirt and bat their eyes when they think that will work in their favor. Mackenzie was just so fucking *cute*."

"Yeah, I remember that from when I pulled her over. But you can't ask a woman out because she says cute shit, Dax."

"I'm not explaining it right, but seriously, TJ, admit it. There was something about her that even you noticed."

TJ nodded. "Okay, I'll give you that. But I definitely want a report tomorrow."

"You know I don't do that shit."

"I didn't mean a blow-by-blow, but give me somethin'!"

Dax finally grinned at his friend. "All right, I'll let you know how it goes."

TJ shook his head and slapped his friend on the back as they walked out of the diner after finishing lunch. "I hope it works out for you, Dax. Lord knows with the shit you deal with on a daily basis, you deserve it."

"Thanks, man, you'll find a woman for you too. I know it."

TJ shrugged his shoulders. "If it happens, it happens. I'm not worried."

Dax climbed into his government-issued vehicle and pulled out of the crowded parking lot. He had one hell of a meeting to get through this afternoon before he could even think more about his date tonight. The Lone Star Reaper, as the press had dubbed him, had struck again.

A sixth body had been found recently and the Rangers still had no reliable leads. They'd called in the FBI, and the lead agent, who happened to be Cruz Livingston, had called a meeting to discuss the particulars of the case. Dax pulled into the parking lot of the San Antonio Police Department, where the meeting was going to take place. Dax was glad Cruz was on the case. It'd be nice to have an officer he knew, trusted, and respected helping him try to figure out what was going on and hopefully they'd close down the case before the fucker killed another innocent woman.

Dax strode into the building and told the receptionist he was there for a meeting with Lieutenant

Quint Axton and Agent Livingston. Dax was shown into a room where Cruz and Quint were already waiting.

"Dax." Quint nodded at him as he entered. "Thanks for coming down. This shit has gotten way out of control."

Dax nodded in agreement. "Cruz and I have had a few conversations already, and we're glad to bring you into the fold. What do you have on the newest case?"

Quint settled back into his seat and shuffled the file filled with pictures and reports in front of him. Finally he found the pictures he was looking for and, with a flick of his wrist, sent them across the table to Dax.

"Same as the others. A call was received with the details on where to find her. Untraceable and short. Voice was unrecognizable because he used one of those voice-altering devices. She was found in a wooden box, buried about five feet underground at the edge of another rural graveyard. Guy's smart, I'll give him that. No one would question a coffin being buried in a cemetery, for Christ's sake."

Dax looked down at the pictures he was holding. The first was of the disturbed ground at a cemetery. The next was after the ground had been dug up with a backhoe, the coffin visible. The third was of the coffin sitting on the ground next to the hole, its lid pried open. The woman inside was in the beginning stages of decomposition. She hadn't been in there for too long. Dax could see her long blonde hair and the clothes she was wearing were still in good shape. Just as with the other victims, it didn't look—at first glance, at least—as if she'd been raped before being put inside the box. She was completely dressed, her clothes were on straight, and she had no visible marks on her body. She was covered in dirt and the fingernails on her hands had bled profusely. She'd obviously tried with every breath left in her to claw her way out of the crude wooden box she'd been entombed inside.

Dax shuffled to the next photos. They'd been taken off-scene: the inside lid of the box had claw marks on it, showing how desperately the woman had fought for her life, the inside of the coffin, the picture taken after the woman's body had been removed, showing body-fluid stains and an empty water bottle. Dax swore and looked up. He hadn't noticed it in pictures of the killer's other crime scenes.

"He put a bottle of water in with this one?"

The FBI agent nodded grimly.

Dax ground his teeth together. The Reaper was getting more sadistic as time went by. He wanted to provide some "comfort" to his victims, even though he knew they'd never get out alive. It was a complete mind-fuck on the part of the Lone Star Reaper. Dax quickly finished looking through the rest of the pictures.

The hole in the ground, tire tracks in the soft grass, the victim lying on the coroner's table. Dax paused. She'd been pretty. She was slender and had a small tattoo over her left breast, some sort of oriental writing. There was a close-up picture of her hands; her nails had been ripped off in her struggles. Dax put the pictures aside and picked up the medical examiner's report.

Dax was impressed with Calder Stonewall's work. He was thorough and impartial. He'd seen some horrible things, but his reports were easily understood, factual, and to the point.

Calder's report said the woman had been killed by asphyxiation; basically she'd run out of air. Her pupils were fixed and dilated. Dax couldn't think of a more horrifying way to die than to be buried alive.

He turned to his friends. "Anything new this time...besides the water?"

"Nothing with the evidence, or the way he disposed of the body, but he *did* send a note this time." Agent Livingston held up a piece of paper. "He sent it directly to the SAPD. Quint opened it and immediately bagged it. The original is being analyzed as we speak for fingerprints and whatever else they can get off of it."

Dax reached for the note, but Cruz held it out of his reach. "He's making it personal, Dax. You're not going to like it."

"I don't like anything this asshole does, Cruz. Let me see it."

Cruz handed over the piece of paper as he waited for Dax to read it.

BY NOW YOUVE FOUND my latest prezent. I hope you like it. Im impressed you brought in both the FBI and the Rangers. I must be doing something right. Im watching you. Agent Livingston, Ranger Chambers and Officer Axton. Your in my sights. You better hold tight to your loved ones.

"YOU HAVE GOT to be shitting me." The words came out of Dax's mouth without thought. "This fucker is threatening us? How in the hell did he get our names?"

"Hell, Dax, you know the papers are all over this shit. They don't give a damn about protecting our identities." Quint's statement was matter of fact.

"Dammit!" Dax didn't have any words. He knew his job was intense, but he never wanted to bring danger to any of his friends in the process. All he'd ever wanted to do was get into the elite Texas Rangers. There were only about a hundred and fifty Rangers in the entire state. There were a ton of specific qualifications an officer had to have to even be able to *apply* for one of the coveted positions. Dax had worked his butt off and loved what he did, but this...this was something he had no experience with.

"Okay, so this guy knows us. Fine. What's our next step?"

"We find out if there are prints or anything else we can go off of on the note. The crime scene guys are examining the coffin. We're interviewing anyone who might have seen anything in the cemetery over the last week and we're telling the public to be alert and careful. *We* also need to be careful. I know none of us are dating anyone, but we need to be sure to alert our families to be extra vigilant until this guy is caught."

"Fuck." Dax knew it wasn't enough. They all knew it was only a matter of time before he kidnapped some other unsuspecting woman and did it again.

Dax thought about Mackenzie. For a split second he considered calling off their date. If the killer was serious about targeting their loved ones, he could easily misinterpret a dinner date and target Mackenzie. Dax dismissed the thought almost as soon as he had it. It was just a date. And he wasn't willing to give up getting to know Mackenzie for a threat that was most likely bogus anyway.

"I'm going on TV tonight to update the public on what we know. We're hoping someone saw or knows something and will call us."

"We're not going to catch this guy with a few random tips, Quint, and you know it," Dax said quietly, frustration lacing every word.

"I know, but we literally have nothing else."

Cruz spoke up. "The FBI has a profiler going over the details and will share a profile tonight. It should hopefully generate some new leads. *Someone* knows this guy."

Dax just nodded his head, lips pursed together tightly. This was the part of his job he hated. He hated waiting for a serial killer to strike once more. Most of the time the only way they could get new evidence was for him to kill again, and that sucked.

"That's all we got for now. I just wanted to bring you up to speed," Cruz told Dax softly.

"What was her name?"

Knowing whose name Dax was asking for, Cruz

said evenly. "Sally Mason. Married with two kids. Twenty-six years old."

Dax shook his head sadly. Such a fucking waste.

"Go home, Dax. We'll be in touch if we hear anything else. You're off for a few days, right?"

Dax nodded. "Yeah. I've worked a ton of overtime lately, so the Major ordered me not to show my face in the office again until next Tuesday."

"Lucky dog." Quint's words were heartfelt.

"But that doesn't mean you don't call me the second you hear anything new on this asshole," Dax warned.

"Ten-four. No worries. I've got you on speed dial."

Dax nodded at Quint and Cruz. "We have to catch this motherfucker."

"We will."

Dax stood, gave each man a chin lift, and walked out the door. He had three hours to get into a better frame of mind before he picked up Mackenzie for their date.

* * *

MACKENZIE PACED her little living room nervously. She'd decided that morning she must've been under the influence of some drug last night when she'd agreed to this date. Hell, she didn't really even *know* this guy, had only seen him once...why in the hell had she agreed to go out to dinner with him? It was absolutely crazy.

Laine had been ecstatic for her, and threatened bodily harm if she even *thought* about calling it off, but Mackenzie was still nervous as hell about it.

She'd picked up the phone to call Daxton to tell him she'd changed her mind and realized she didn't even have his number. He'd called her yesterday from a blocked number. Mackenzie had thought about bailing and going somewhere outside of her apartment until way after six so she wasn't home when Daxton got there, but she couldn't. That would be really rude, and she hated to be rude. Besides which, she'd never hear the end of it from Laine if she did something so cowardly.

So here she was, going on a date with a man she didn't know, had only lusted after, and seen briefly through tears in the rear-view mirror of her car and at the charity benefit event and who knew way more about her than she knew about him. Crazy.

Mackenzie rubbed her hands on her thighs, trying to calm herself down. She could do this. It was just a date. That's all. Dinner. If she could keep from dropping or spilling anything on herself, or Daxton, she'd be fine. He'd see she wasn't anything special and bring her home and she'd never see him again. No problem.

Mackenzie was wearing a faded pair of jeans with a pair of black flip-flops with a small heel. She'd always loved them, even if her feet usually hurt by the end of the day. She wasn't used to wearing heels at all, but she figured she'd need every inch of the two inches in height they gave her.

Her shirt was a basic black short-sleeved pullover with a scoop neck. Nothing fancy, and she'd purposely chosen black so if she did drool on herself, which was likely with her track record, it wouldn't show as easily. The shirt did show off her breasts though. Her chest was one of her best assets, and she hadn't met a man yet who could resist checking it out.

Mackenzie had pulled her hair back in a twist and secured it to the back of her head with a barrette. She knew by the end of the night it'd probably mostly be falling out, but for now she thought it looked okay.

She continued to pace until her doorbell rang. Mackenzie looked at her watch. Dang, he was right on time. He was one of *those* people. Mackenzie couldn't manage to be on time if her life depended on it...although today was apparently an exception. She'd been ready for half an hour, a record for her.

Mackenzie walked over to the door and looked through the peephole. Damn. The man standing there was so good-looking, she felt a zing shoot through her body, ending between her legs. She'd gotten the same reaction the night of the charity event. He was looking directly at the peephole, as if he knew she was on the other side looking at him. Mackenzie took a deep breath and opened the door until the chain stopped it from opening any farther.

"Daxton?"

"Yup. That's me."

Mackenzie shoved her hand through the small opening of the door and said, "ID please."

Dax chuckled, not offended in the least. "Good girl." He reached behind him, took his wallet out from his pocket, pulled out his driver's license and put it into Mackenzie's outstretched hand. "There you go."

Mackenzie looked down at the plastic card in her hand. Daxton Chambers. Forty-six years old. Six feet one and two hundred thirty pounds. She gulped. Damn, almost a hundred pounds heavier than she was. She went to hand it back and dropped it.

"Shit, sorry."

Dax just laughed quietly and kneeled down to pick up the license. "No problem."

Mackenzie held out her hand again. "Ranger ID now, please."

Dax smiled even more broadly. "Damn, woman."

Mackenzie faltered a bit, but bravely said, "IDs are easy to fake nowadays, I just want to make sure."

"Oh, I wasn't complaining. No fucking way. I'm pleased as hell you don't trust me. I'd be more worried if you did. Good thinking. Here you go." Dax held out his Texas Ranger badge that he'd pulled from his other pocket. "I don't go anywhere without it, just in case." She took it from his hand and Dax could see her hands shaking.

"If it's okay…I'll just—" Mackenzie gestured back inside her apartment.

"Take your time, Mackenzie. I'll be right here."

Mackenzie shut and locked her apartment door and quickly walked over to her phone. She snapped a picture of Daxton's Ranger badge and texted it to Matthew, Mark, and Laine. Laine knew she was going out with Daxton, but she wanted to inform her brothers as well. She told them she was going to dinner with Daxton, who was a Texas Ranger, and she'd be back later. She trusted Daxton was who he said he was, but she wanted her brothers to know who it was she was going out with and what time she expected to be home. Even though she was thirty-seven years old, she wanted to be safe. She'd call Laine after the date. It was their ritual whenever one of them went out.

Mackenzie thought hard about calling the local Rangers' office and checking on Daxton that way as well, but then decided she was being an idiot. She'd seen him at the charity event with a table full of other officers. Hell, he'd been with the Highway Patrolman when she'd been pulled over. If Daxton was lying, he was an expert. Mackenzie went back to the door, took off the chain and opened it all the way.

"Hi, Daxton. It's great to meet you." Her smile was bright and welcoming, as if this was the first time she'd opened the door that night and she hadn't demanded he show his IDs to her and treated him like a criminal.

Dax chuckled. Damn, she was charming. She pulled him out of his bad mood easily. "Hey."

"Here's your ID back. Sorry about that."

"Don't be sorry. You have no idea how hot that was."

"Uh, what?"

"Yeah, hot. I see all sorts of shit in my line of work. I love knowing you're cautious. I just wish more people were like you."

"Oh, well, okay." Mackenzie handed Daxton his Ranger ID.

"What'd you do with it when you were in there?"

"Uh…" Mackenzie was unsure if she should tell him. "I don't know…um…I've never dated a cop before."

Dax stood there watching Mackenzie with an amused glint in his eye. "Okay."

"And I've never been in trouble before. I mean, really in trouble. I got detention in high school once, but it wasn't my fault. Stupid Darci Birchfield decided to pick on one of the guys on the chess team and I told her if she didn't lay off him she'd answer to me, and she didn't lay off him, so she answered to me and I got a full week of detention for it. But she never messed with him again. I had to endure Bobby thanking me for the rest of our high school years, and shit, he *still* sends me a Christmas card every year, but still…it was totally worth it."

Daxton leaned against the wall next to the door, loving how fucking cute she was. He crossed his arms over his chest, holding his cowboy hat in one hand, and settled in to listen to Mackenzie babble.

"Okay, I also got in trouble at work last year for telling one of the other managers to go fuck himself, but *that* wasn't my fault either. He was totally harassing one of the lesbian women I work with. Calling her a dyke and shit like that. That's just not cool. I mean really, in today's day and age, that crap is totally uncalled for. So I told him off, explaining how a dyke was actually an artificial wall used to regulate water levels, and called a levee here in the States. Okay, I probably also used some other not-so-nice words as well, but he turned around and complained to HR about *me*, when *he* was the one being an asshat. I was sent home for a week, paid, while an investigation was conducted, but was called back after only three days because Ginger totally told HR what a dick Peter was and that I'd been defending her, and since everyone in the office backed Ginger, they ended up letting Peter go and not me."

Mackenzie paused, biting her lip. Shit. She'd done it again. She tried to finish her thought quickly. "So, I've never really been in trouble, or even been around any cops, other than the charity thing each year, so I have no idea what's legal and what's not, so I'll tell you what I did if you promise not to arrest me. I'm claiming ignorance here."

"What'd you do, Mackenzie?" Dax asked with no animosity in his voice.

"I took a picture of your ID and sent it to my brothers and best friend so if I end up dead in a ditch somewhere tonight, they'll know who it was who took me out. I totally planned on deleting the picture when I got home, though. It's not like I was gonna put it on the Internet for someone to make a fake ID from or anything."

"Good for you."

"Really?"

"Yeah. But you know, that name could be totally fake. If I *did* want to kill you and dump your body, and your brothers or friend checked me out, they might not ever find me if I used a fake name."

"Damn." Mackenzie liked this guy. "So what should I have done instead?"

"Called the Ranger Station and checked me out. Told them you're about to go on a date with a man who claims to be a Ranger and that you have a badge and you want to know if it's legit or not."

"I totally was going to do that!" Mackenzie exclaimed excitedly.

"Why didn't you?" Dax asked.

"Well, because it felt like a shitty thing to do...not trusting you when you gave me your ID without giving me crap about it."

"Do it now."

"What?"

"Do it now. Call. Check me out."

"But you're standing right here. And I believe you."

"Do it." Dax's voice was unrelenting.

"Oh all right. Jeez." Mackenzie turned to head

into her apartment and pick up her phone she'd left on the counter—

When her arm was suddenly grasped tightly and pulled behind her back and she was turned and pushed up against the wall in her hallway.

Mackenzie looked up at Daxton in surprise and with a little fear. "What the hell?"

"Don't turn your back on someone you've just met, Mackenzie. If I wasn't who I said I was, I could have you flat on your back by now. You're such a little thing, you wouldn't be able to move, and I could do anything I wanted to you. I could tie you up and haul you out to my car. Don't *ever* let anyone get you in their car. Yell, scream, fight. Your chances of survival drop by fifty percent if you let yourself get taken away."

Mackenzie could feel her heart thudding in her chest. Daxton was holding her against the wall with one of her wrists held tightly behind her back. He'd crowded in until he was pressing against her with his body, holding her immobile. One of his legs was between hers, holding her completely immobile.

The top of her head came to about his chin and she had to tilt it back to look into his eyes. Daxton was wearing a polo shirt with the top two buttons undone. She could see no chest hair, but she could smell him. He was wearing some sort of cologne, nothing too strong, but it smelled divine. Mackenzie knew it was entirely inappropriate to want to bury her nose into the hollow at his neck, but damn.

Mackenzie's breasts rubbed against Daxton's chest as she breathed in and out and she could feel her heart pounding. God, had she ever felt this way in the arms of any of her previous lovers? Hell no. And she and Daxton were both fully clothed.

She wiggled against him, testing his hold on her. It was solid. Her free hand gripped the shirt at his waist tightly, wondering what his next move would be.

"Are you listening to me?"

"Uh…yeah?"

Dax laughed and brought the hand that had been holding her shoulder to the wall to the side of Mackenzie's head. He looked down at her semi-glazed eyes and smiled. "You aren't afraid of me." It wasn't a question.

Mackenzie shook her head.

"Why not? I could do everything I just told you without breaking a sweat."

"Because a bad guy wouldn't tell me those things, he'd just do them." Mackenzie didn't know how she was conversing in a normal way with Daxton, when all she wanted was for him to do the things he'd just described, including throwing her down on the ground and having his way with her. "And you called me 'little.' I've never been described that way by anyone in my entire life."

"Fuck." Dax couldn't help himself. He leaned down and placed his lips over hers. Brushing over them once, then again, this time sweeping from one side to the other with his tongue. When she opened her mouth under his and touched her tongue to his bottom lip, he straightened up before things could go any further. Mackenzie's lips were soft and tasted slightly of apples. Daxton felt ten feet tall. He wasn't alone in whatever this weird attraction was.

"Go make that phone call, sweetheart. I'll wait right here." Daxton slowly let go of Mack's wrist he was holding behind her back.

"Okay." Mackenzie made no move to leave the hall.

Dax took a step back, pulling Mack with him. He then turned her physically with his hands on her shoulders and gave her a little push at the small of her back. "Go on."

Dax waited in the hall by her front door as Mackenzie went back into her apartment. He heard her on the phone doing just as he'd told her, apparently learning he really was a Texas Ranger and his legal name really *was* Daxton Chambers. She came back, this time carrying her purse and a light jacket.

"Okay, Daxton Chambers. You came back clean. You're good."

"It's Dax. You can call me Dax."

"Is it a deal breaker?"

"Is what a deal breaker?"

"I like Daxton. I don't know; you don't look like a Dax. Not that I've ever met anyone named Dax or Daxton before though. You'll have to tell me how you got that name. That's another reason why I figured you were who you said you were. No one would call himself Daxton if he was using a fake name to get a woman to date him. He'd call himself John Smith or something. Not some sexy-as-hell name like Daxton fucking Chambers."

Mackenzie looked up at the strangled sound Daxton was making. "Fucking hell. Sorry."

"Do you know, I've laughed more in the last twenty minutes than I have in the last week? Don't be sorry. And yes, you can call me Daxton."

"Does anyone else call you that?"

"No."

"No? Not even your mom?"

"Nope, and my parents passed away ten years ago."

"Oh shit, I'm sorry. There I go again, putting my foot in my—" Mackenzie's words were cut off when Dax put his hand over her mouth.

He leaned in close. "It's fine. I like my full name coming out of your mouth. I like it a hell of a lot."

Mackenzie waited, holding her breath. Was he going to kiss her again? The brief touch of his lips earlier made her girl parts sit up and take notice. She hadn't thought she'd be that easy, but apparently three years with only her vibrators for company made her ripe and ready for this man.

Dax took his hand off Mack's mouth and said easily, "You can call me Daxton if I can call you Mack."

"Only my family and friends call me Mack." Her voice was low.

"Since I want to be your friend…now I do too…if that's okay."

"Yeah, it's okay."

"Great. Now shall we go?"

"Where are we going?"

"It's a surprise."

"Really?"

"Yeah, Mack. Really. That a problem?"

"No, not at all. But no one has ever taken me on a date before and not told me where we were going."

"I'm glad I'm your first." Dax laughed as Mackenzie blushed. "Damn, you're cute. Come on, I'm starved. Let's go."

Mackenzie locked her apartment door behind

them and followed beside Daxton as he led the way to his car. It was nothing special; in fact, it blended in with all the other cars in the lot quite easily. It was a black four-door Ford Taurus. It was almost a shame. A sleek sports car seemed more his speed. Daxton held the passenger-side door as Mackenzie got in and then shut it behind her once she was safely in the car.

He walked around the front of the car quickly and settled into the driver's seat. He pulled on his seat belt and turned on the engine without a word. He backed out of the space he'd parked in and headed out of the neighborhood.

"So…" Mackenzie's voice was hesitant. She had no idea what to talk about.

"So…" Dax echoed.

"You've laughed more tonight than you have in the last week?"

Dax glanced at Mack. She'd turned so her back leaned against the car door and crossed her legs. She'd put her purse on the floor in front of her and was watching him with her head cocked. Dax liked how all her attention was on him. She wasn't asking to be polite; it honestly looked as if she cared what he had to say.

"Yeah, I can't talk particulars, but the cases this week have sucked."

"The Lone Star Reaper?"

Dax looked sharply at Mack again, showing his surprise at her comment.

"Daxton, I'm not an idiot. Every time I turn on the TV, the news is talking about it. I know another woman was found this week. He's been the leading story for the last month or so. Hell, I think I remember them saying there was a Special Response Team that had been assigned to the case. I don't know if you're on the case or not, but I just assumed you were. I'm sorry if you want me to be a good little girl and not ask about that shit, but I can't be. I might not know anything about the police, but when this story is in the news every damn day and I'm a single woman, I can't help but pay attention."

It wasn't funny, but Dax struggled to keep from smiling anyway. Mack was so easily riled. It was a good thing he wasn't. "Sorry, Mack. You're right. I don't think you're an idiot. And yes, the case has been weighing on my mind a lot this week."

"Okay, I know this is our first date and all, but I'll listen if you want to talk about it…at least what you can."

"Thanks, but no. Can we agree to put all talk of work behind us for the night? I'd rather get to know you than talk about that asshole."

"Deal."

Dax did smile at that. So far, Mackenzie was perfect. He enjoyed being around her, and enjoyed talking to her. She was funny and didn't seem to care about saying the "right" thing, but preferred to blurt out whatever she was thinking.

He also enjoyed her body. He was a man, after all. Holding her against him had solidified that. She was soft in all the right places. Looking down at her while he'd held her in her front hall was almost painful. He'd tried to be careful not to pull her into him too closely; otherwise she'd have felt for herself how attractive he found her. Having her breasts rub against him was one thing, but if he'd pulled her hips into his, it would've been obvious how much he enjoyed holding her against him.

Dax had about lost it when he'd looked down and seen her little nipples tight under the black shirt she was wearing. Because he was so tall, he could practically see down her shirt. He'd known it was rude as hell, but seeing her breasts pushing up into the scoop neck of her shirt made him want to squeeze them in both his hands. They were obviously more than a handful, and he wanted nothing more than to learn the feel, texture, and taste of them.

Fuck. He had to concentrate, otherwise he'd get hard again. Not something Dax wanted to do on their first date. He thought about a safe topic of conversation.

"Okay, so if we're getting to know each other, tell me about your family."

Mackenzie rolled her eyes. "You would start off there, wouldn't you? Okay, but don't blame me if you decide to ditch me at the nearest street corner when I'm done."

Dax could hear the laughter in her voice and merely shook his head at her and gestured for her to continue.

"So, you know I have two brothers, Mark and Matthew—"

"Wait."

Surprised at Daxton's interruption, Mackenzie halted immediately. "What? What's wrong?"

"You have two brothers named Mark and Matthew? And your last name is Morgan...and your name is Mackenzie?"

Seeing where Daxton was going, Mackenzie laughed. "Yeah, apparently my parents thought it was trendy to have the M theme carry on throughout all their kids."

"Do their names start with M as well?"

"Of course." Mackenzie chuckled at the incredulous look on Daxton's face. "Myra and Milton Morgan. So anyway. I'm the middle kid. Matthew is forty and Mark is thirty-five. I'm sure we were a handful, being so close in age. We're all pretty close. My dad died three years ago of a heart attack. It was sudden, and we miss him a lot, but we're doing okay. I get together with my mom and brothers at least every other week. They love me a lot, but don't really understand me. I'm stubborn and they think I'm way too picky. My mom wants me to get married and hurry up and squeeze out a gazillion grandbabies for her."

"Are your brothers married?"

"Yup, and they each have three kids. You'd think the six grandkids she already has would be enough for my mom, but nope. She wants more. I really like my sisters-in-law, who, by the way, don't have names that start with M. Salena and Kathy are great, but we aren't that close."

"What doesn't your family understand about you?"

Mackenzie tried to get her thoughts together to try to explain what she meant without sounding like a complete loser or headcase.

"And don't hold back now. Seriously, tell me what you're thinking."

"I'm thinking I want you to like me, Daxton, I don't want to chase you away on our first date."

Dax took his right hand off the steering wheel,

placed it on Mack's knee, and squeezed briefly. "Mack, I already like you. I go through my day talking to people who are only telling me lies. When they get caught in one lie, they tell another to try to get out of it. I have to dig and dig to try to find out the simplest things. You have no idea how refreshing it is to me that you don't play any games…at all. You lay it all out there. At this point, nothing you can say now will make me not want to see you again. Okay?"

"Even if I said I had the hots for my brothers' wives?"

"Okay, maybe that." Dax smiled at Mack again and put his hand back on the steering wheel, even though he wanted to keep it on her knee, and waited for her to continue.

"I'm picky. I like things done a certain way and I'm stubborn. I think when I start dating a guy, I wonder about what *he* thinks about *me*, and it freaks me out. Am I chewing too loud? Do my clothes look okay? Should I wear more makeup or less? And you might have noticed I have a bad habit of blabbering on and on about nothing. So after I stress when I wonder what he might be thinking about me, I start to find things wrong with the way *he* does stuff and I call him on it. Incessantly. Until he can't take it anymore and he leaves."

Mackenzie decided she'd rather Daxton end this

now once Dax knew how she really was, than fall in love with him and have him leave.

"Holy shit."

The words came out without Mackenzie meaning them to. What had she just thought? Had that been her problem all along? That wasn't really what she was going to tell him, but now that she thought it, she couldn't *un*think it.

"What?"

"I..."

"What, Mack? Go on."

"I think I've pushed guys away in the past because I knew it'd hurt less for them to leave me before I fell in love with them and they decided to leave anyway."

Instead of the censure Mackenzie was sure would be sent her way, Daxton's voice was level and understanding. "That makes sense. You must have been hurt that way in your past."

"Are you a mind reader?" Mackenzie asked, only half kidding.

Dax chuckled. "No, sweetie, but I don't think you're all that abnormal. Most people want to protect their hearts. It's never any fun to love someone and have them leave you anyway."

"Did that happen to you?" Mackenzie asked before she could think about it.

"Yeah."

"I'm sorry, Daxton. That sucks."

"Yeah. I fell head over heels in love with her and had planned the rest of our life all out in my head. I got a promotion and was supposed to move from El Paso to Austin. Stupidly, I accepted the job without consulting with her about it. I know it was a dick thing to do, but I honestly thought she'd be thrilled for me. She knew how hard I'd been working for the promotion, and she even knew I'd flown to Austin to interview. But when I told her I accepted the job, she flatly refused to leave. She grew up in El Paso and all her family was there. Ultimately, she chose them over me."

"What a moron."

Dax just shook his head and smiled. Mack never said what he thought she would.

"I mean seriously. To give you up for her family? It's not like her family would disown her or anything if she moved…wait…would they?"

"No, they wouldn't have."

"Right then, so she made you choose between her and your career. Sorry to say, but you made the right choice, Daxton. I know I've been a bitch to some of the men I've dated, but I never, not once, made them choose between their job and me. Besides, look where you are today. You're a Ranger! I don't know anything about anything, but I've heard how the newscasters talk about you guys and I don't live in a hole, I know about Rangers. You're amazing! There's no way I'd choose my brothers over you, I mean, seriously. I love them and all, but why would I give up a hot guy and great sex for the rest of my life for my *brothers*? No freaking way! And another thing..."

Mackenzie was on a roll and didn't even seem to notice how Dax's body had gotten tight upon hearing her words.

"She couldn't have loved you. Not really. Not a real true-to-the-marrow-of-your-bones love. If you had that kind of love, there's no way she would've made that decision. Yeah, I get it. El Paso and Austin are far apart, but it's not like they're in different countries."

Mackenzie's voice softened for the first time since her tirade. "If she truly loved you and knew it was what you wanted and what was best for you, she would've moved with you in a heartbeat. It sucks to hear that, I'm sure, but I believe it. Shit, even though you aren't married, I still think you made the right decision. What if you'd married her and tried to make it work and she pulled the same kind of thing later? You'd be stuck in a job knowing you could've had better and would regret not taking the Austin job. That would eat at you and you'd be miserable. So yeah, that sucks, but I think you're better off."

Mackenzie looked up at Daxton, startled because the car wasn't moving anymore. They'd pulled into a parking lot and Daxton had cut off the engine. He was staring at her with a weird look on his face.

"Shit, I overstepped, didn't I? Dammit, I told you I was like this."

"No, Mack, you didn't overstep. You're right. It *was* probably for the best."

"I didn't mean to insinuate that you didn't love her."

"I know you didn't."

Mackenzie closed her eyes and put her forehead in the palm of her hand. "My family also says I have a tendency to talk too much."

"You don't talk too much, Mack. Promise." Dax leaned over and pulled Mackenzie toward him with one hand behind her neck. He kissed her on the top of the head and leaned back. "Ready for some food?"

"Yes, please. Food sounds good. Anything at this point, other than me going on and on about your love life, sounds good."

"Come on then. I hope you'll like this place." Dax had already thought all the things Mack had said at one time or another, but the fact that'd she'd immediately been able to sum up all the reasons why Kelly and he didn't end up together was very insightful... especially for them just having met. It boded well for their budding relationship; at least what he hoped was a budding relationship.

Mackenzie looked up and saw they were at a restaurant on the south side of the city she'd never been to before. Mood lightening, embarrassing conversation forgotten, Mack exclaimed, "Oooh, I've always wanted to eat here!"

"Good. Today's your chance."

Dax exited his side of the car and started to walk around to help Mack out, but she met him before he'd gotten half way around the vehicle.

"I know, I was supposed to wait for you to come open my door, right? I can't. Sorry, Daxton, but seriously, I don't get that. I'm just supposed to sit there with my hands in my lap waiting for you? I feel stupid just sitting there like a helpless little woman. I have two hands. I can open the door just fine by myself."

"It's the gentlemanly thing to do."

"I know, I *know*, but I still think it's weird. I mean, I know you're a gentleman. Hell, the entire embarrassing episode at my apartment told me that."

"How about we make a deal?"

"What kind of deal?"

"The kind of deal where if I tell you it's important to me to come around and assist you out of the car so you don't fall over or when I want to be a gentleman, you'll agree. And if I don't bring it up, you can get out on your own and meet me here, in front of the car, just like you did today."

Mackenzie thought about it for a second and smiled, liking that Daxton thought there'd be times in the future they'd be driving somewhere together. She liked it a lot. "Okay, deal. If it's important to you, tell me and I'll wait. Otherwise I'll do my own thing."

"Good, let's go." Dax took Mackenzie's hand and laced their fingers together, liking the feel of her hand in his. He had a good hunch about Mackenzie and dinner. He hoped this was the beginning of a long relationship.

CHAPTER 6

THE CAR WAS silent on the way back to Mackenzie's apartment after dinner. Dax had a great time, Mackenzie was a hoot, and he couldn't remember when he'd enjoyed a date more. Granted, he hadn't been on many dates in the recent past, but he still didn't think any of them had been as fun as this one had been.

The restaurant was one of Dax's favorites. It was a cross between a bar and grill and a diner. Around ten each night, the owners stopped serving food and the ambiance changed to more of a bar-type atmosphere.

Dax and Mackenzie had eaten, then sat talking until Mack suggested they play darts. The funniest part was that she'd never thrown a dart before in her life. She was awful at it, but she laughed at herself every time she missed the bull's-eye by a mile.

And Mackenzie *was* clumsy. She hadn't been lying. At one point, she'd reached across the table and knocked over his water glass. She'd apologized profusely, but Dax had waved it off. Since the seat on his side of the booth had been wet, it'd given him an excuse to move over to sit next to her, so it had all worked out in his favor anyway.

Then when they were playing darts, she'd dropped one and it barely missed landing on her foot. One throw also went way wide and luckily had bounced off the wall and landed on the floor, instead of about a foot to the left, to the man standing next to the wall drinking a beer. Mackenzie decided she'd had enough darts at that point.

They'd laughed and Mack had giggled as their date continued. She hadn't been pissed or thrown a hissy fit when a woman, out having drinks with friends, came up to him and gave him her business card and said, "Call me." Mackenzie had thought it hilarious instead.

It was a refreshing change from the last woman Dax had dated, who'd been pissed when another woman had slipped him her phone number while they were out on a date one night. Even though he hadn't done anything to encourage the waitress in any way shape or form, his date got upset at *him* and insisted that he must've done something to make her think he was into her. It was the last time Dax had asked her out.

Now Dax was taking Mackenzie back to her apartment. He didn't want the night to end, but it was late and Mack was yawning in the seat next to him. He pulled into the parking lot and turned off the engine. Dax waited until Mackenzie turned to look at him.

"Wait there, I'll come around." He paused until Mack smiled and nodded at him.

Dax went around the car, opened the passenger door, and held out his hand. Mack put her hand in his and allowed him to help her up and out. Dax held Mack against him as he shuffled them out of the way so he could shut the door. He could feel her heat through the light jacket she wore.

"Thanks for letting me help you. It's dark. It makes me feel better to have my hands on you as we head for your apartment. Okay?"

"Yeah, okay."

"Come on, let's get you inside."

Mackenzie smiled as Daxton led her across the parking lot to her door. She'd had a great night. "I almost ditched you, you know," she told Daxton out of the blue.

Dax smiled. "Yeah?"

"Yeah. I was going to call you and let you know I'd changed my mind, but I didn't have your number, you had it blocked."

"Yeah, I don't like my number out there, especially when I'm following leads on cases."

"I get that. Anyway, then I thought I'd get out of my apartment and wait for six o'clock to pass, then go back home, but I knew that'd be rude and Laine would've kicked my butt. So I decided I'd just tell you when you arrived that I didn't want to go, but I couldn't do that either. So I took a chance. I've only been on one other blind date in my life, and Laine set us up, so I felt pretty safe. The only other time in my life I took a chance that huge was when I moved here to San Antonio. I was living in Houston and got the job offer here. It's not like I make a ton of money, but I knew it'd bring me closer to my family, so I did it. It scared the hell out of me at first, to have to move and make new friends and stuff, but in the end, it turned out all right. Then luckily Laine decided she missed me too much and she moved here, too."

Dax knew he'd never tire of Mack's rambling way of talking to him. It was cute as hell. She had no idea how much information she gave him with her seemingly unrelated ramblings. He loved it. "So,

I take it you're not sorry you took the chance on me?"

"Uh, no." Mack said it as if she was saying "duh". "I was a bit freaked that I didn't even really know you. I mean, I saw you at the charity event and thought you were hot as hell, but I didn't *know* you. I've only been on one blind date before, and it was a disaster. And you know, some cops are assholes. I would've been so disappointed if you were one of those, but so far, you've been cool. I've never really liked the whole cowboy-hat thing; I mean a cowboy hat is just funny looking. A lot of men can't pull it off, but on you? I'll just say, you can pull it off just fine. And you're in shape. I'm sure you know that, I mean, you see yourself naked all the time, and I haven't, but seriously, I can tell you're muscular as hell and don't have a beer belly. Why don't you? I mean, you drink beer, you had one tonight, but you're not fat at all."

Dax's lips twitched as he tried to keep his laughter inside. They'd arrived at Mackenzie's door. He turned her so her back was to the door and he was towering over her. He caught Mack's hands in his and brought them up to his chest. He placed her palms flat on his shirt and pressed, indicating she should keep them there. He then framed her face with his hands and tilted her head up.

"You approve of my body, Mack?" He was amused to note that she seemed speechless for the first time tonight. "Because I sure as hell approve of yours."

At the roll of her eyes, Dax continued.

"You fit me perfectly. You're a little thing next to me, and all I can think about is caging you in my arms and having my way with you." He watched Mack swallow.

"Uh…"

"And your curves have been driving me crazy all night. There's nothing sexier than a woman with curves. When I stood behind you tonight and helped with your form as you tried to throw that damn dart, you have no idea how hard it was for me not to push myself up against you to show you how I felt about your hips, and legs, and tits."

"Uh, seriously, Daxton…"

"And your mouth. Hell, woman. Watching you talk to me tonight, watching you lick your lips when they were dry…it took all my willpower not to haul you over the table and into my lap and lick your lips myself."

Dax paused, enjoying the flush that came over Mack's face and her shifting movements against him, before continuing.

"I've had a wonderful time. Not only do I like

your delectable little body, I like what's inside it. I've enjoyed talking to you. You're refreshing, especially compared to my friends and the criminals I talk to day in and day out. Don't ever change."

"Uh. Okay."

"And I want to see you again. I'm going to give you my number so you can call me—not to blow me off, but because you want to talk to me. Because you want to know when I'm taking you out again. Because that's what you do with the man you're dating. You good with that?"

"We're dating?"

"Yeah, we're dating."

"Oh. Okay."

"Good. So first things first. I'm going to kiss you. I'm going to taste those lips again. That one taste I got before we left wasn't enough, and I'm going to make it the best kiss you've ever received. After that, I'm going to let you go, because I know if I don't, I'll haul you inside and take you in your hallway until I empty myself inside you and can't stand up anymore. You good with *that*?"

Mackenzie stared up at the man in front of her in bewilderment. He'd been fairly easygoing all night. He was certainly an alpha man, but he hadn't really let it show until just now. Mack flexed her hands until her fingernails were digging into the shirt over his rock-hard chest.

"I'm not sure why you see all that in me, but I'd be an idiot to disagree with you. I'd also be lying if I said I didn't want the same thing. Please, Daxton. Kiss me before I have to tackle you to the ground and have my wicked way with you."

Dax smiled. "You've managed to keep me on my toes all night tonight, Mack. Hold on to me."

He leaned down, tilting Mack's head back even more as she tried to keep eye contact. She really was tiny compared to him. Liking the power he had over her, just because of his height, Dax swooped down and took her lips with his, without any preliminaries. He plunged his tongue inside her mouth and loved it when Mack immediately countered his thrust with her own. There was no way she'd ever just lie under him and take whatever he wanted to give her. She'd fight to give it right back.

Dax moved one hand from the side of her head to the small of her back and hefted her up against him until her feet left the ground and they were touching from groin to chest. He felt her wrap both hands around his neck to help hold herself up. She tilted her head to the side to give him greater access as he continued his onslaught on her mouth.

He sucked her tongue into his mouth and bit

down gently. Dax could feel Mack shift against him restlessly and one of her legs came up hesitantly beside his hip. She couldn't hold it there, but tightened her hold on his neck.

Dax thrust his tongue back into Mack's mouth and took his time learning each and every contour and memorizing the taste and feel of her. Finally, knowing he had to stop, or he wouldn't be *able* to stop, Dax drew back and leaned over to put Mack back on her feet. He moved to lick at the corner of her mouth, he nipped at the side of her jaw, then sucked on her earlobe before moving down to her sensitive neck. Dax felt goose bumps rise against her skin as he licked and nibbled at a sensitive spot.

"Uh, Daxton, I've never had a one-night stand in my life, I'm just not the kind of girl who can imagine something so intimate with someone I don't really even know. But I think you should be aware; I'm seriously reconsidering the type of girl I am right now." Mackenzie's voice quivered with the intensity of her lust.

Dax smiled against Mackenzie's skin, running his hands up and down her spine and backside. He finally lifted his head to look down into Mack's eyes. "We aren't rushing this, Mack. There's no need for a one-night stand. This is gonna last a hell of a lot longer than one night anyway. Let go of me and let me give you my number."

Mackenzie realized she hadn't let go of him since he'd put her on her feet and she reluctantly forced her fingers to unclench at the back of his shirt, and to lower her arms. She licked her lips, liking how Daxton's eyes followed her movements.

"Give me your phone, Mack."

Mackenzie reached into her purse and pulled out her cell. She entered the password and put it into Daxton's hand. She watched as he clicked buttons as he added his contact information.

"I programmed in my cell, my work number, as well as the number at Company F...which is my Ranger Company. If you can't reach me, leave a message. If it's an emergency, call the company and tell them it's you. I'll make sure the admins know you're with me and if you call, they can interrupt me. They can get in touch with me no matter what I'm doing. Okay?"

"Wow. Okay, but I'm not the kind of woman who needs to call if she runs out of milk or something, Daxton. I can go and get the damn milk myself. You should get that about me."

"And I'm not the kind of man who expects or wants you to call me if you've lost your purse. But I *do* expect if you truly need me, that you'll call. I won't be happy to find out you've driven yourself to the emergency room or clinic if you fell and broke something."

"Really? That's the example you have to give me?"

Dax liked her spunk. "Yeah. You were the one who told me you were clumsy, remember?"

"Okay, okay, you're right."

"Good. So you'll call."

"Yeah. I'll call if I need something. But, Daxton, you should know something."

"What's that?" Dax fingered the hair by Mack's ear that had come loose from her clip and was wisping around her face.

"I'm a text kinda girl. I have the unlimited package. I like texting, sending and receiving. Is that a problem?"

Dax smiled and leaned down and kissed her hard, and way too briefly, before pulling back. "It's not a problem. I'll get used to it."

The smile he got in return was worth his response. Dax knew he'd do what he could to see it again and again. "Okay, I'm really going now. Lock your door and stay safe."

"You'll…" She paused, not sure if she'd sound too needy if she asked what she was thinking.

"What, Mack?"

"You'll call? We'll go out again?"

"Fuck yeah. I said we were dating, I didn't lie. We're going out again."

When he didn't say when, Mackenzie mentally shrugged. "Okay."

"Okay. Inside. Lock the door."

"Thanks for a fun night. I'll talk to you later."

"Yes, you will. Good night, Mack."

The last thing Mackenzie saw when she shut the door was Daxton's upward chin lift as he stood and watched, making sure she barricaded herself inside her apartment. She slid down with her back to the door. Her butt landed on the floor and she wrapped her arms around her drawn up knees. She smiled. Holy freaking hell she was in trouble.

CHAPTER 7

"DON'T BE NERVOUS, ma'am. Just tell me what you remember seeing that afternoon." Dax tried to sound calm and reassuring. Interviewing witnesses was a delicate balance between being sympathetic, but pushy, when it came to trying to pry the right information out of them.

"I'd gone to the cemetery to lay flowers on my dear Harold's grave and I saw a big tractor digging a hole in the back corner of the lot. I thought it was odd because that part of the cemetery hadn't had a funeral held in it in a long time, but what do I know about how cemeteries do business? Maybe they were starting a new plot."

"What color was the tractor?"

"Yellow."

"Did it look old? New? Did you see anyone?"

"Well, I don't know my tractors, but it was very shiny. There was someone in the cab, but I couldn't see him at all. The windows were tinted and it was so far away."

"What time was it?"

"It was around three in the afternoon. I remember because I had a hair appointment at three thirty and I didn't want to be late."

"Thank you, Mrs. Sutton. You've been a big help." And she had. They knew the killer used a yellow tractor and the time he buried his victim. Dax would check with the cemetery staff and see if it was theirs. If they were lucky, it wasn't, and they could do a check of the Department of Motor Vehicles on anyone that owned a yellow tractor. He'd also be sure to tell Cruz to alert the caretakers of the local cemeteries to be on the lookout for any unusual activity in their areas. The local police agencies could also increase patrols around the rural cemeteries as well. It wasn't fool-proof, after all they hadn't been able to catch this guy yet, but it was something. The killer hadn't called in to brag about this victim until apparently a week after he'd put the coffin in the ground. The timeline fit what Conor had said about time of death.

"Do you think you'll catch him? What a terrible man, to do those things."

"Yes, ma'am. We'll catch him. We're doing everything possible to catch him sooner rather than later."

"Well, thank you for what you do, young man. The world needs more people like you in it."

Dax helped the woman out of the chair and to the door. "I advise you to keep your visits to Harold at a minimum, at least until we catch whoever this is. If you need to visit, don't go alone."

"I can do that. I'll have my son, David, come with me next time."

"You do that. Thanks again, Mrs. Sutton." Dax nodded at the woman as she left his office. He sighed and sat back down in his chair and looked over the pictures strewn in front of him. Dax had heard back from Cruz. The FBI analysts hadn't found anything useful on the note the killer had sent. There weren't any usable fingerprints and the only trace evidence that had been on the note was a single hair, which seemed to have come from a cat.

So Dax had a lot of information, but it was all disjointed. Their killer was a man who owned, or had come into contact with, a cat, he either owned a yellow tractor or had the know-how to hotwire one. The coffins were a dead end because they were homemade. They could try to track the hardware used to assemble them, but that was a long shot. Fuck. They had information, but it still seemed like they were still at square one.

The phone on his desk rang; it was Quint from the San Antonio Police Department.

"Hey, Dax. Got time for lunch today?"

"Actually, Mack is supposed to come to my office today for a quick lunch, want to join us? I can ask her to pick up an extra sandwich on her way in."

"Sure, if you don't mind."

"Yeah, I've actually been wanting you to meet her anyway. I know it's soon, but I really like her."

"You seem serious about this one. How long have you been seeing her?"

"I *am* serious about her. It's been about two weeks."

"Great, what time then?"

"How about twelve fifteen?"

"See you then."

Dax put the phone back in its cradle and leaned back with his arms behind his head. He knew Quint probably wanted to talk about the Reaper investigation, but Dax needed some Mack time before he'd be able to dive back into the horror that was the case. Burying women alive was some sick shit and Mack helped him keep everything in perspective.

The two weeks since they'd been dating had been great. They'd met up several times for dinner and had advanced their kissing at her door to kissing in his car, and even once on her couch while they were watching a movie.

Dax was trying to take things slow, but the more time he spent with Mack, the more he knew in his gut she was the woman for him. He'd been instantly attracted to her, but it wasn't just that he wanted her sexually. She was funny. She was polite. She didn't get riled up when something went wrong, it just rolled off her back. During one of their dinners, she'd bumped the plate the waitress was clearing from their table and a full cup of ranch had spilled down the front of Mack's shirt. Mack had merely laughed. Dax shook his head remembering. Mack had almost bent double guffawing at herself and how clumsy she was as she dabbed at her shirt trying to mop up the mess. She'd been more concerned about the waitress, who'd been absolutely mortified. Mack had smiled and told the poor waitress it was an accident and it was fine. Of course they'd gotten their meal free, along with a complimentary T-shirt from the restaurant, but Mack hadn't been upset in the least.

Mack also wasn't afraid to admit when she screwed up, something Dax had rarely seen in the women he'd dated in the past. She laughed at herself when she tripped over nothing, or dropped something. She really was accident prone, but it didn't seem to faze her. It was refreshing to be with a woman who said what she thought most of the time, but still wasn't quite as confident in her own skin as she might try to portray to the world. It was that dichotomy that drew him to her. She also didn't seem to be full of the drama that so many women were these days, which was a relief.

Dax had been on a lot of dates, and had even thought he'd loved a woman once or twice, not including the woman he'd almost married back in El Paso. He'd participated in a couple of one-night stands, and usually felt used. But Mack, she was different. He felt it to the very marrow of his bones.

Mackenzie hadn't lied that first night they'd gone to dinner. She did have a habit of trying to boss him around and make him do things the way she wanted them done. They'd had dinner at her place one night and she'd spent ten minutes lecturing him on the best way to wash dishes. For the most part, Dax went along with it, because he honestly didn't give a shit if he put the dishwasher soap on the sponge thingie or directly on the dirty dish when he was washing it, but apparently, Mack did.

However, he called her on some things. When he did, Dax could see her stop and really think about them and the times she gave in seemed to cement his feelings for her all the more. Mack wasn't being unreasonable for the sake of being unreasonable. Dax hoped the fact that she'd occasionally back off something she wanted done her way, and let him do it however he wanted, meant she liked him and was really trying to make their relationship work.

Like the time she pulled out her credit card to pay for dinner one night. Dax had told her that as long as they were out together, whether it was at a restaurant, gas station, or a department store, she'd never pay.

Mack had puffed up like a banty rooster and had insisted and cajoled and pouted, but in the end, when he'd explained that it made him feel like less of a man when she paid, she'd caved. Of course, later that night she'd told him in no uncertain terms that if he *wasn't* with her, and she was buying food, or whatever, for both of them, *she'd* pay for it. Dax had tickled her unmercifully until giving her what she needed…his agreement. Compromise was the backbone of any relationship and Dax loved that Mack was sincerely trying to compromise for him.

Dax didn't really mind that Mack wanted to pay

her way; it was actually refreshing. His relationship with Mack was a complete one-eighty from his relationship with Kelly, the woman who refused to move to Austin with him. She'd never paid for anything, never even *offered* to pay for anything. She'd always expected Dax to pay for everything, from the rent and electricity to the credit cards she'd maxed out. Looking back Dax knew he'd been a sucker, but he'd honestly believed she was the woman he'd spend the rest of his life with.

Dax quickly texted Mack and told her Quint would be joining them for lunch and asked her to pick up a third sandwich. She texted back immediately—another thing Dax loved about Mack, she never made him wait and wonder if she got his message—and agreed without a fuss. She was text crazy, as she'd warned. But it kept the communication open between them, and even Dax had to admit it made him feel good inside to know she was thinking about him when she sent random silly texts just to say hi.

An hour later, Dax heard a knock on the door.

"Come in."

Mack sauntered into his office with a smile on her face and two large bags in her hand.

"Hey, Daxton. How's your day been?"

"Better now that you're here. Come here, sweetheart."

Mack plopped the bags on the little table off to the right of Dax's desk and went to his side, shrieking when he pulled her into his arms in the chair.

Mackenzie immediately straddled Daxton's lap, fitting her knees into the small spaces next to his hips.

"How come you never wear a skirt?"

Mackenzie scrunched up her nose in disgust. "Ugh. I hate them."

"Why?" Even as Dax asked, he knew he'd get an earful. Sometimes he purposefully asked her things that he knew she'd ramble on about because he loved to hear her talk.

"Because they're sexist. I mean really. Back in the dark ages, it was the *men* who wore skirts...or togas or kilts, or whatever they were called. *Their* legs were sticking out, showing off their knees, exposing their backsides if they fell over. Sometime in the last thousand years, some *man* came to his senses and decided he'd rather see a woman's knees and backside."

"Thanks for the history lesson, Mack. Now...why do you really not wear skirts?"

Mackenzie smirked at Daxton. "Do you know, I actually like this position. I can look you in the eye and don't have to worry about you getting a crick in your back from leaning down to me, and I don't have to worry about getting a cramp from looking up at you."

At his raised eyebrow, Mackenzie sighed, knowing she'd been trying to avoid answering his question. "So there was this one time right after I graduated from college and had my first job. I was extremely proud of myself and felt very professional. I bought myself a bunch of new suits to wear to work. I thought I looked very sharp. The first day of work, there were three men who, when they met me, looked me up and down and their eyes stayed fixated on my legs. The second day, I had a woman tell me, politely, that if I needed help shopping for professional clothes she'd be happy to go to the mall with me to pick out more appropriate clothes. On the third day, when I was wearing my favorite of the three skirt sets I'd bought especially for my new job, I slipped in the lobby. My legs went flying out from under me and my skirt came up around my waist as I fell and gave everyone standing around a cooter shot. I heard the security team had it on the security cameras and passed it around to everyone in the company. That was the last time I wore a skirt to work."

"That shit is illegal."

Mackenzie put her hand on Daxton's cheek, not in the least perturbed at her story, or at his ire. "I know. I turned them in and HR fired everyone who they could prove participated in the sharing of the video."

"I should've known you wouldn't have let that pass."

"Of course not. Assholes. That was the last time I wore a skirt to work. I'm just too clumsy to risk it again. Not to mention I don't need anyone making me the butt of their jokes because they don't think I've got the right kind of body to wear a short skirt."

"Wrong," Dax rebutted immediately.

"Huh?"

"You're wrong, Mack." Dax's hands went from resting at her waist down to her ass and he hauled her closer to him. Close enough that he knew she could feel his erection up against her woman bits. "You have the perfect body for wearing a skirt. Imagine if you were wearing one now. Think about what we could do during our lunches together if you wore one every day."

Mackenzie didn't hesitate, but shoved her hands next to Daxton's body until they were resting over his shirt under his arms. She leaned in and whispered, "Daxton, you think a pair of pants would really prevent me from taking you in this chair and riding you until we were both piles of goo if I really wanted to?"

"Hello!"

Dax and Mackenzie both jerked in surprise and turned to the door. Quint stood there, one hand on the doorjamb, smiling at them.

Mackenzie laughed and moved her arms out from Daxton's sides. Dax reluctantly eased Mack back a bit so she wasn't pressed up against him and took his hands off her ass. "We'll continue this conversation later," Dax whispered before returning Quint's greeting.

"Hey, Quint, it's good to see you."

"Uh-huh, sure."

Dax smiled at his friend and helped Mack to her feet, steadying her when she stumbled. "Come over here and let me introduce you to Mack, otherwise known as Mackenzie."

"It's nice to meet you, Quint," Mackenzie said politely, holding out her hand.

"I think the pleasure's all mine." Quint brought Mackenzie's hand up to his mouth and kissed the back of it.

Daxton reached up and took Mackenzie's hand

out of Quint's. "Enough, Quint."

Quint laughed. "It's just too easy. So...how did you guys meet again?"

Dax opened his mouth to give his friend the short version when Mackenzie piped in.

"Well, I saw him for the first time at that charity event over a month ago. We didn't really meet there though, we just talked briefly. Then I was speeding because I had a crap day, and Daxton's friend pulled me over. But he was nice enough to ignore the fact I'd had a crap day and was crying my eyes out, and gave me a warning instead."

"I don't know what that story has to do with meeting Dax here," Quint said in confusion.

"Oh, well, apparently they were on their way to dinner when I zoomed past them and Daxton was in the car with the Highway Patrol guy and he saw my license, realized he'd met me at the charity thing, called to make sure I was all right after being pulled over and then demanded I go to dinner with him. He came over, I embarrassed myself, as usual, and we went out. He kissed the hell out of me on my doorstep and now here we are."

Quint smiled in amusement and looked at Dax. "How come I didn't see her at the charity thing? Dammit, you Rangers always get the good ones."

Dax laughed and pulled Mack over to him and

kissed the side of her head, refusing to rise to Quint's bait. "Hungry, sweetheart?"

"Starved."

Dax loved that Mack wasn't afraid to show that she was human and hungry. Too many women he'd been around tried to pretend that a leaf or two every other day was enough to live on. "What'd you get us?"

"I got you a turkey and cheese sandwich with all the trimmings—yes, including jalapenos. I still don't know how you can eat those, but whatever. I got myself a BLT, minus the mayo and double the T, easy on the B. And I didn't know what your friend would want, so I got both a ham and cheese with the normal condiments, and I also went outside the box, in case he was like you, and ordered a meat-lover's sandwich with every kind of meat and topping they had. Chips for all of us and waters as well."

"Will you marry me?" Quint asked with a smile and his hand over his heart.

Mackenzie giggled at him and rolled her eyes. "Whatever."

The trio settled themselves at the small table and Mackenzie passed out the sandwiches, smiling when Quint chose the meat-lover's sandwich. She knew Daxton would eat the ham and cheese later. It seemed as if he had a bottomless stomach; he could always eat.

After they'd made small talk for a bit, Quint broke the lighthearted mood.

"The Lone Star Reaper struck again."

Mackenzie gasped and Dax put down his sandwich abruptly. "What the fuck, Quint? Not in front of Mack."

Mackenzie put her hand over Daxton's on the table. "It's okay, really. I'm actually interested."

Dax looked at Mack closely, seeing she was serious, and didn't seem concerned at all. He looked back at Quint and warned, "Nothing deep, got it?"

"Yeah." Quint understood what Dax meant. He'd keep the talk general and not share any of the extreme details until he could talk to Dax alone. "He called it in again, he didn't write a note. She was found on the north side of the city, again in a small rural cemetery. She was buried off to the side as usual, not in the main part of the lot."

Mackenzie interrupted, her curiosity overcoming her reticence to butt into the conversation when she didn't really know Quint. "So this guy kidnaps women, then buries them alive? Right?"

"Right."

"Why?" Her question was short and to the point.

"What do you mean, why?" Quint asked seriously.

"I mean, what does he get out of it? Are the women raped?"

If Quint was surprised at Mackenzie's question, he didn't show it. "No, not as far as the medical examiner can tell."

"So, why is he doing it?"

"Well, besides being an asshole, we aren't sure, Mack," Dax answered, picking up Mackenzie's hand and playing with her fingers absently. "We can't find any connection between the women at all. As far as we can tell, they didn't know each other. They didn't live in the same part of the city. They all had different jobs. We can't find the connection."

"Okay, but again, I guess I'm confused about why he's doing it."

"Who knows why any psycho does the things they do?" was Quint's response.

Mackenzie's brow furrowed in concentration. "But there has to be a reason. Nobody does things without having a reason. Is he pissed at the government? Was he abused as a child? Does he have Mommy issues? Why? If he's not raping the women, he has to get something else out of it. When I was in middle school, I remember a kid kicking a stray dog. I confronted him about it and asked what the dog had ever done to him to deserve to be kicked. The kid said he'd been bitten by a stray dog when he was younger and hated them ever since. So okay, I didn't like his answer and told him he was an idiot, but my point is, he had a reason to want to kick every stray dog he saw. I know that's way too simplistic and I don't mean to say that every guy who has ever been hurt or dumped by a woman would turn into a serial killer, but I still wanna know what *this* guy's reason is."

"Fuck, Dax. If she wasn't already yours—"

"She is." Dax cut off Quint's words immediately and continued as if he and Quint didn't have the short but intense side conversation. "We don't know, Mack. The profilers have some guesses, but we don't really know why he's doing it. We're trying to find out why he's burying the women alive. If we can do that, we might be able to search the databases and find out who he is."

"I suppose it can be hard to really figure out why anyone does anything nowadays. I mean, why do I harp on Daxton when he insists on putting the knives in the dishwasher with the points up? I know it's better to put them pointy side down so you don't cut yourself when you're emptying the stupid thing, but Daxton just can't seem to get that. I mean really, if he wants to risk stabbing himself every time he puts anything in or takes anything out, that's on him, but ultimately it's really not a big deal. Right?"

Dax leaned over and kissed Mack on the side of the head, as he was wont to do. "Right, sweetheart." He leaned back over to his seat and picked up what was left of his sandwich.

"Well, the first time you slice your palm when you're emptying the dishwasher, you'll see I know what I'm talking about."

Quint and Dax both laughed at her and they finished their lunch.

Dax walked Mack to the door and turned back to Quint, knowing he wanted to speak to him alone as much as Quint probably wanted to speak to him. "I'll be back in just a sec."

"I know you need some time to talk to your friend without me there, Daxton, I'm sorry I was in the way," Mackenzie said in a low voice as they got to the door.

"You weren't in the way."

"Well, I hope you know that I realize your work comes first. So if you have to text me at the last minute and let me know you need to cancel, that's okay. Even if I've already picked up lunch, I can find someone who will eat it. Hell, I swear the people I work with are professional mooches. I never leave anything in the fridge there anymore because it'll disappear faster than ice cream on the Fourth of July. All I'm saying is, I know what you do is important and that you can't talk about some of it with me, and that's okay. Hell, I don't *want* to know the details on most of the things you do, but I've been on my own for a long time now and won't be hurt if you have to do other things instead of eat lunch with me."

"Come here, Mack." Dax pulled Mackenzie into his arms and leaned down to her. "You're amazing."

Mackenzie smiled. "Naw, just too old to get sucked into the drama shit that happens in a relationship when two people don't trust each other. I trust you'll let me know if I drive you crazy or if you don't want to see me anymore."

Dax leaned up and looked Mack in the eyes. "That's not gonna happen anytime soon."

"Okay."

"Okay. Be safe today. I'll talk to you later."

"I had a nice lunch. I like your friend."

"Me too, Mack. And as long as you like me better than him, I'm okay with you liking Quint."

"I like you more than him," Mackenzie reassured him with a smile.

Dax kissed Mack hard on the lips and set her away from him. "Get back to work, sweetheart."

Mackenzie waved as she turned around—and ran

right into one of the other Rangers who was coming in the door. Luckily he caught her by the arms before she fell over.

"Sorry! Shit, sorry!" She smiled sheepishly at Dax and was gone.

Dax simply shook his head, realizing he'd happily spend the rest of his life catching her when she tripped over her own feet, or someone else's, and headed back to his office to see what it was that Quint wanted to tell him about the Reaper case.

Quint didn't waste any time. "This one had a walkie-talkie in the coffin with her."

"What the holy fuck?" Dax's mellow mood from spending time with Mack disappeared in a heartbeat.

"Yeah, the batteries were dead, and when they were replaced in the lab, it wasn't on a channel that would connect with anyone. The best we can figure, the Reaper wanted to be able to talk to her, or for her to be able to talk to someone else. We have no idea if it actually worked or not so far though."

"Has the next of kin been notified?"

"Not yet, we're still working to identify the victim."

"Fucking hell. He's escalating. He wants to torture his victims. If he's the one talking to them, he can say all sorts of shit to them while they're dying.

If he wants them to be able to talk to someone else… what's his purpose behind that?"

"It's as your Mackenzie said, we have to find out why. Find out what his trigger is."

As much as he liked the words, "your Mackenzie", Dax's mind was stuck on this latest development from the psycho targeting helpless women. "I'm on it. I'll look again and see what I can find in the records for boys ages five to fifteen and see if I can't find something, anything, in someone's past that might trigger something like this. It's an extreme long shot though, and we'll probably get more from surveillance of the cemeteries, but it's worth a shot. I'll get in touch with Cruz and see if he can't hurry up the profilers to give us more to go on."

"Good idea. We're gonna catch him, Dax," Quint tried to reassure his friend.

"I sure hope so. This could keep getting uglier and uglier if we don't."

"I like Mack." Quint changed the subject so abruptly, Dax had a hard time switching his mental gears.

"I like her too."

"She's spunky and quirky and down-to-earth."

"I know."

"You're a lucky man. Don't fuck it up."

Dax smiled for the first time. "I'll try not to."

"You do that. You gonna eat that ham and cheese sandwich, or can I take it?"

"You touch it, you die."

Quint merely laughed. "Okay." His voice turned serious. "Let me know what you find. I don't have a warm and fuzzy feeling about this."

"Will do. Me either."

CHAPTER 8

THE LAST MONTH had been quiet; at least, the Lone Star Reaper had been quiet. Other cases, of course, took precedence, so it wasn't as if Dax was sitting around doing nothing all day, but there had been no more dead women found buried alive in coffins, and the Reaper hadn't communicated with anyone at all.

Dax didn't like it. He preferred action over inaction. He felt in his gut the Reaper was still out there killing, he was just biding his time before bragging about it.

Daxton and Quint had gotten with Cruz and he'd hooked them up with the profilers in the San Antonio office of the FBI. After many hours of research and discussion, they finally had a profile.

The Lone Star Reaper was most likely a man in his mid-thirties, unmarried, and a loner. He'd probably be highly intelligent, but not with a high education. He most likely went through some sort of psychological abuse when he was a child. He'd likely experienced a head injury when he was young, which affected the pre-frontal cortex, the area of the brain that controls judgment. The profile also suggested that he lived and worked in San Antonio and had probably had several blue-collar jobs throughout his life.

Further analysis by the profilers revealed that the Reaper probably had a domineering mother who was very strict and a father who wasn't around. He most likely had never had a steady relationship with a woman, and if he had, it was almost certainly dysfunctional.

The profilers warned that he undoubtedly had an unnatural fascination with death, perhaps even attended funerals and visitations of people he'd never met. He may or may not be concerned with his personal grooming habits, and therefore could have dirt under his fingernails from the burials. It'd be a reminder of what he'd done, and he'd like that reminder. The Reaper would also in all likelihood be what most people would consider "strange" or "weird."

The communications liaisons from the FBI and the Rangers had teamed up to go on the local news to share the profile. Since then, every law enforcement agency in the greater San Antonio area had been busy fielding phone tips about every weirdo people believed could be the killer. Hell, even the Highway Patrol officers were on the lookout for men who fit the profile when they pulled anyone over.

So far nothing had panned out, and the fact that the Lone Star Reaper had gone quiet didn't sit well with Daxton, Quint, Cruz, and every other officer in the city. Everyone was simply holding their breath waiting for the next body to be found. It wasn't a good feeling, knowing someone had to die in order to get more clues to the killer's identity.

The best thing going on in Dax's life was his relationship with Mackenzie. He was more than ready to move it to the next level. They got along great, she made him laugh, and every time his phone dinged, letting him know he'd received a text, he hoped it was from Mack. She'd gotten in the habit of texting him throughout the day to tell him completely random stuff. He loved it.

He picked up his phone when he heard the signal letting him know he had an incoming text.

Would it be inappropriate if I throat punched my boss?

Dax laughed out loud, thankful no one was around to hear him. He typed out a quick response.

Yeah, most likely. And you probably shouldn't tell your Ranger boyfriend you are considering assault and battery.

Expecting Mack to respond right away, Dax was surprised when it was over an hour before he heard from her again.

Okay, you can't do that shit to me, Daxton.

Concerned, Dax texted back immediately.

What shit?

Tell me you're my boyfriend.

Dax smiled and typed out a quick response. *Wanna go steady?*

She responded with, *Do you like me? Check Yes ___ or No___*

Dax loved Mack's sense of humor. She never ceased to surprise him.

Where's the 'Hell Yes' box?

Dax's phone rang not too much later after his last text. "Hey, Mack."

"Don't you think it's too soon?"

"What's too soon?"

"For us to be labeling what we have as boyfriend and girlfriend?"

Dax got serious. He thought this might be coming. "Mack, we've been out every weekend since we met. I can't count the number of dates we've had, because we've had too many. One of which ended with both of us on your couch, me with one hand down your pants and the other under your bra. I've had my tongue practically down your throat every time we've seen each other and you've inspected every inch of my bare chest with your hands *and* your mouth. Did you seriously just ask me if it was too soon for us to be calling each other boyfriend and girlfriend?"

"Daxton!"

Dax smiled, knowing Mack was blushing. "Mack!"

"Okay, yeah, you have a point, but I just...we haven't...I don't know what this is."

"You're coming over tonight, yeah?"

"If you still want me to."

"You're coming over tonight. Bring a bag. You're staying the night." Dax could hear her breathing, but she didn't say anything. He eased his tone back a bit. "Mack, I want you to stay the night. If you're not ready for more than what we've done, no problem. I want to hold you in my arms as you sleep tonight, sweetheart. I've spent too many days in my shower thinking about you in my bed and jacking off. Sorry if that's too crude, but it's the truth. I want you in my arms. It's time."

"I sleep naked." Mackenzie blurted out the first thing that came to mind after his words.

"What?"

"I sleep naked. I always have. I don't like the feel of a shirt or pants on when I sleep. I don't sleep calmly. I toss and turn and my clothes always end up wrapped around me and I feel like I'm being strangled. I'd like to say I'll try to put something on, something sexy and lacy, but I can't, it's just not comfortable. I'm sorry. I know it's weird, but I've always been that way."

"Mack—"

"And it's weird that we haven't even slept together yet and I'm blurting this out, but I don't think I can spend the night. It'd be weird if I wasn't ready and you wanted me to sleep over and I took all my clothes off. It wouldn't be fair to you, I'd be leading you on or something, and I don't want to do that. I'm not a tease and I don't want you to think that I am."

"Mack, seriously, shut it, I—"

"And, you have a fourteen-pack. Seriously, you work out every morning and all I want to do in the mornings on the weekends is lay in bed until like ten. I hate working out, and I know I should, that would help my love handles, but I get all sweaty and gross then I'm sore and I'd rather keep my body the way it is—a bit big, but okay—than work out and hate every second of it."

"Mack, swear to God, shut up and listen to me."

Dax's words seemed to echo across the connection. Mackenzie swallowed and bit her lip. "Sorry, Daxton. Shit. Sorry…go ahead."

"I'm not sure even where to start after all that, but here goes. I wasn't kidding when I told you I jacked off to the thought of you. I have and I do. I wanted you the second my tongue touched yours in your apartment that first day. Your nipples got hard against your shirt and I looked down at your tits and got an erection. I'm forty-six, Mack, I don't spontaneously get hard anymore. But looking at you? Thinking about easing into your hot folds? Yeah, I'm hard right now just talking about it. Mack, I love your body. It's not perfect, but whose is? You know what? I hate my legs. Seriously, my abs and arms are good, but my legs have always been too skinny. I can't bulk them up no matter what I do. I'm telling you this so you know that we all have hang-ups about our bodies."

Dax took a deep breath and pushed hard on his erection. Fuck, he was hornier than he could remember being in a long time.

"I wish you could see how hard I am listening to you talk about how you sleep nude. Fuck, woman. Thinking about you spread out on my sheets, naked as the day you were born, you have no idea what that visual is doing to me. I swear to Christ, if you aren't ready, I'll be as good as a choirboy. You aren't a tease. You're about as far from a tease as any woman I've ever met. You say exactly what you're thinking all the time. You let it all hang out. I never have to guess what you're thinking. That's my favorite thing about you. Seriously. So please, come over tonight. Stay the night. Sleep naked in my bed, in my arms. If we make love, we make love. If not, it's okay. We'll get there when we're both ready and not a moment before."

Dax waited a beat and when Mackenzie didn't respond, he said, "Mack?"

"My family wants to meet you."

Dax laughed again. "See? You don't hold anything back. And I want to meet them too, sweetheart."

"But it's weird. My mom called last night and browbeat me for twenty minutes until I agreed to bring you over next week for dinner."

"Okay. That sounds good." Dax let Mack talk, let her work through his words at her own speed.

"My mom likes flowers; you'll have to get her some. Don't let Mark and Matthew badger you into saying anything you'll regret later."

"No one bullies me into saying anything I don't mean, Mack. No one."

She finally worked herself back around to his

earlier words. "I want you to touch me. I want you inside me, Daxton. I've dreamed about it too. My vibrator has had more action since we've been seeing each other than it's ever had before...and I'm not ashamed to admit that's saying something. I lie in bed naked at night wishing you were next to me, but not knowing how to make that happen. If I asked you to stay, I'd feel like a slut. Hell, not a slut, it's not like I put out...at all...but it'd be weird. But I swear, just about every night I get myself off thinking about you."

Dax sighed in relief. He'd gotten what he wanted. Loving the thought that she'd gotten herself off while thinking about him, but knowing he couldn't go down that road while he was working, he changed the subject. "You want me to pick you up tonight, or will you meet me at my place?"

"Will you pick me up?"

"Of course. I'll be there around five thirty. Will that give you enough time to get home and get ready after work?"

"Yeah."

"Okay, I'll see you then. And Mack...no pressure. Okay?"

"No pressure. I'll see you later, Daxton."

"Later, sweetheart." Dax hung up the phone and smiled, not knowing how he'd make it through the rest of the day. It was bad enough he woke up with a hard-on every morning, but he didn't want to walk around the Ranger Station as he was right now.

Dax put his head back on his office chair and tried to think about something other than Mack naked in his bed.

CHAPTER 9

Mackenzie shifted nervously and turned to face Daxton. "Thanks for dinner. It was delicious."

"You're welcome. You're easy to cook for. You eat anything I make, no matter how awful it is."

"That's not true. I didn't eat the rolls you made that one night."

"That's because they were completely black on the bottom and I almost burned the place down."

Mackenzie smiled at Daxton and changed the subject abruptly. "I'm nervous."

Dax leaned over and hauled Mack into him. He leaned back against the sofa and cradled her in his arms. "I know you are. You have no reason to be, but I know you are."

"I'm not fifteen. I've done this before. I know how it all works, but I'm still nervous."

"It's our first time, Mack, I'm nervous too."

"You are?"

"Yeah."

"You shouldn't be."

Dax smiled. He knew she'd say that. "One time in my early twenties, I thought I was all that and a bag of chips. I sauntered into the bedroom, completely naked, ready to impress my girlfriend, and she took one look at me and started laughing hysterically. I had no idea what she was laughing at. She couldn't even breathe, she was laughing so hard. I lost my erection and went back into the bathroom to put my pants back on, humiliated. It wasn't until I was removing the condom that I'd put on in preparation of our night that I noticed it was glowing. I'd accidentally grabbed one of the novelty condoms I'd picked up at a bar earlier that month. I'd walked into the bedroom ready to impress her, with a glow stick attached to my body. No wonder she laughed."

Mackenzie giggled at the picture Dax put in her head. "It still wasn't nice of her to laugh at you like that."

"I deserved it."

"Even so, I wouldn't laugh at you."

Dax pulled Mack closer into his body and leaned down so he could speak right into her ear. "One of the things I like most about you, Mack, is your ability to laugh at yourself and at me when I deserve it. My job isn't the happiest in the world, but I've found myself smiling more at random times of the day when I think about something you've said or done than I ever have before. So laugh at me, laugh at *us*. It's all good. Because I know you. I know you're not laughing *at* me. Even if I do something stupid, you're still not laughing maliciously *at* me. You'll laugh, then share the joke with me so I can laugh too."

"Glow-in-the-dark condom? Got any more of those?"

"Sorry, I'm fresh out...but I do have some of the regular ones."

"Thank you."

"For what?"

"For not making this weird. For bringing up the subject of condoms so I don't have to. For wanting me. Just...for all of it."

"Mack, we're not teenagers anymore, birth control isn't something to be embarrassed about. I don't know about you, but I'm not sure I want to have kids this late in life. I'm not ready to say 'never' just yet, but we both know it's too early to even have that conversation together."

"I'm on the pill. I started it when I was sixteen and my mom dragged me down to her doctor and told him to 'get me started.' It was embarrassing for both of us, but it was the right thing to do. I've never gone off them. I don't think we'll have to worry about babies."

"That's good, sweetheart. But I'm still going to use protection for our peace of mind."

"I haven't slept with anyone in three years."

Dax watched as Mack's blush went from her ears down into her shirt. He moved one of his hands to her stomach and under her shirt until it rested on her bare skin.

"Three years?"

"Yeah. At first I was just busy. I didn't really think about it much. I had my...toys...and wasn't interested in men too much anyway. Then when I did get interested again, I couldn't find anyone who fit the bill. I mean, I know I'm getting older and my prime time is ticking away, but I couldn't find the energy that was required to put into any kind of relationship. It all seemed so pointless anyway."

"Then you met me."

"Then I met you." Mackenzie agreed softly.

Dax moved his hand even farther up under her shirt until it rested directly on her breast. He ran his thumb rhythmically over the side of her soft mound over and over until he felt her nipple come to life under his hand.

"I'm clean, Daxton. I'd tell you if I wasn't."

"I know you would, Mack. I'm clean too, but it hasn't been three years for me. I'll wait until I can get in to a see a doctor to make sure. Believe me, there's nothing I want more than to get inside you bare. I've only had sex without a condom a handful of times, but somehow I know with you, it'll be nothing like my other experiences. I can't wait to fill you up with my come and watch it slide out of your body when I pull out."

Silence surrounded them for a while, until Mackenzie broke it.

"Okay, I'm just going to throw this out there and you can do with it what you want...I'm not that good at sex."

Dax's hand at her breast stopped moving, and Mackenzie hurried on. "I mean, I can do the basics, but I've never been able to orgasm very quickly or easily, and that's irritated men in the past. Usually, I end up getting the guy off and then worrying about myself later. Or I'd be with a guy who thought he could 'get me past my issues' and he'd be all cocky and think that he could bring me to orgasm without any problem. Then when he couldn't, it somehow became my fault...so when I told you I was nervous earlier it wasn't just because this will be our first time. It's because I know I'm not good at it, and I want you to enjoy it, enjoy *me*, more than I've ever wanted to please anyone before in my life. But I'm scared you'll be disappointed."

Dax moved before Mackenzie could figure out what he was doing. She was on her back under him as he pressed his hips into hers. His head was higher than hers since their hips were lined up, and Mackenzie had to tilt hers back to see him.

"I have no doubt we'll be good at this together, sweetheart. No pressure. Seriously. If you can't orgasm with me, we'll experiment with your toys. We'll get you off first, then me. Or I'll go first, then take care of you. It's not a contest. I hope like hell I can watch you explode in my arms, but if not, we'll figure it out together. What do you fantasize about?"

"Huh?"

"Fantasize, Mack. What are your fantasies? What do you think about when you're using your vibrator?"

Mackenzie looked anywhere but at Daxton. She shouldn't be embarrassed. Sex was a normal thing, a healthy thing, but it was still awkward.

Dax put his hands on Mack's waist and slowly brought them upward, taking her shirt with it. "Arms up." She immediately moved, allowing him to tug her shirt off over her head. Dax looked down and put his hands on her breasts, caressing and squeezing as he spoke. "What positions have you made love in? Did one position feel better than another? What about erotic pain? Has anyone pinched your nipples as they were pleasuring you? Have you tried anal play? Some people are more sensitive than others back there and it can bring a lot of pleasure if done right. Do you like to tell your lover what to do or have him tell you what to do?"

"Are you going to let me answer any of those questions or are you going to keep firing them at me all night?"

"Sorry," Dax said with a sheepish grin. "Just thinking about doing those things with you made me lose my mind for a moment, Please, carry on."

"If I can remember what you asked correctly… doggy and missionary, no, don't know, no, no, and the latter not the former."

Dax smiled down at Mack and pulled her bra down under her breasts. Without looking away from her face, he took both nipples in his hands and pinched lightly until Mack squirmed under him. "Do you like that, sweetheart?" At her nod, Dax let go, rubbed his palms over her nipples, then took them between his fingers again, pinching harder than he had before, until Mackenzie arched into him, moaning and digging her fingernails into his biceps. "I'm not into pain myself, but there's something to be said for a little bit of…discomfort to make you concentrate on the pleasure."

Mackenzie's hands moved up his arms to grip Daxton's wrists. She wasn't stopping him, but she had to hold on to something. "Daxton…"

Dax's gaze left Mack's for the first time and looked down at his hands. "I love the way you say my name, and fuck, you are beautiful. Seriously. Look at these beauties. Your nipples are red and standing straight up, begging for my touch. Your breasts are soft and fleshy and I can't wait to hold them together as I thrust between them. I can feel you squirming under me, are you wet, Mack? Does this feel good?"

"You know it does."

"You aren't going to have any problem getting off with me, sweetheart. I'm not being arrogant like the other men you've been with. If I can make you squirm with just my hands on your nipples, I can make you come. I promise you that." Dax let go of her breasts, leaving her bra where it was, pushing up her mounds. He stood up and held his hand out. "Come on. It's time."

Mackenzie swung her legs to the side and let Daxton help her up.

"Come up here." Dax held Mack by the waist and urged her to jump up into him. She didn't hesitate and hopped up and wrapped her legs around his waist. Her naked breasts were sensitive and she squirmed against him as they rubbed his shirt as he stalked out of the TV room

Dax walked with one hand under Mackenzie's ass and the other holding her at the small of her back. When he got to his bedroom, he put her down by the bed and said simply, "Strip."

Dax could tell Mack was unsure, but she immediately put her hands behind her back and unhooked her bra, letting it fall to the ground. Her hands then moved to her pants and undid the button and unzipped them. Without breaking eye contact with Dax, she pushed until they fell to a heap on the floor and she stepped out of them. Mackenzie put her hands to the sides of her panties and Dax took a step toward her.

"Let me."

Mackenzie's hands froze and she pulled them away from the cotton at her hips.

Dax put his own hands where hers had just been, but he hesitated, saying in a low, reverent voice, "Fuck, sweetheart, you are my ideal woman. Look at you. Lush and curvy. Breasts that overflow when I hold them. Soft skin that pebbles under my hand." Dax ran his hand up Mackenzie's side then back down, proving his words true as goose bumps rose on her skin everywhere he touched. "No matter what happens tonight, I'll always remember this moment. You, standing naked next to my bed for the first time, giving yourself to me so unselfishly, even though you're unsure."

Dax eased his hands under the cotton on the sides of her hips and slowly pushed down, not taking his eyes away from her for a second. Suddenly dropping to his knees in front of her, Dax held her in place with one hand while he pushed her underwear to the floor with the other.

Mackenzie took a deep breath. She didn't mind being naked usually, but Daxton's gaze was intense and she could feel herself growing wetter. She jerked in surprise when Daxton leaned forward and put his forehead on her belly. She looked down. All Mackenzie could see was the top of Daxton's head. His nose was…right there. She moved to step back and Daxton's hands tightened on her hips.

"Don't move, sweetheart," he mumbled into her flesh. "I'm soaking up the moment here."

"Daxton—"

"Shhhhh."

Mackenzie giggled, she couldn't help it. "Okay, don't mind me. I'll just wait for you to finish…soaking."

Her giggle cut off when Mackenzie felt Daxton's

fingers graze over the hair between her legs. "Holy mother of…"

"You trim yourself down here."

It wasn't a question, but Mackenzie answered anyway. "Yeah."

His hand moved lower.

"And you shave down here. I can feel how wet you are. You're coating my hand with your juices. Fuck, Mack." Dax lifted his head and looked up at Mackenzie. "I want to touch you. I want you to come for me, but even if you don't, I can make sure it feels good for you, so no pressure. I want to learn you from the inside out. Touch you. Feel you. Taste you. But I won't if it doesn't feel right or you don't want it. We'll climb in the bed and simply hold each other all night. Your choice, Mack."

"I want you."

"Good."

"Can you please get naked now?"

Dax laughed and stood up slowly, running his hands up her sides as he did. Mackenzie could feel her own wetness being spread on her skin as his hand made its way upward. It should've been weird, but instead it was sexy as hell. She *felt* sexy as hell.

"Get on the bed, Mack. Tonight we'll probably keep it simple, but I plan on introducing you to a whole new world of positions later."

Mackenzie smiled as she sat on the mattress and then scooted back until she was in the middle of the bed. She watched as Daxton tore off his shirt, not even trying to prolong it or make his striptease sexy. He undid his belt and didn't bother taking it out of his pants. He unzipped and unbuttoned and suddenly he was standing there completely nude. He'd pushed his boxers down with his pants. He stepped out of the material and, without taking his eyes off of Mackenzie, lifted one leg, and took off one of his socks. He did the same to the other foot and suddenly he was on the bed with Mack.

"I can tell you with one hundred percent honesty that I have absolutely no desire to laugh right now."

Dax smiled and crawled up Mack's body until he was hunched over her on his hands and knees. "Like what you see, sweetheart?"

"Is the Pope Catholic?"

A laugh burst out of Dax. "Fuck, I love that you can make a joke right now. Lie back. Let me make you feel good."

Mackenzie did as Daxton asked. She lay back and pulled a pillow under her head. She knew she'd never forget this moment. She wanted to watch every second.

"Put your hands over your head and don't move them. This is my job right now. I don't need your help. You don't have to do anything, or think about anything but how I'm making you feel. Relax, sweetheart." Dax nodded in approval as Mack slowly raised her arms and put them over her head. He bent his head and nipped the side of Mack's breast. Running his hands over her body as he continued to move downward, he kept up a running commentary.

"Your body was meant for my loving." He squeezed both breasts in his hands as he nuzzled her belly button. "I can hold on and feel *you*, no matter what my mouth may be doing." Dax moved his hands down to her belly, caressing and massaging. "You aren't skinny, you're right, but this is so fucking sexy. I love your body. You're so soft."

Then finally, Dax's mouth was over her folds.

His thumbs moved down to hold the lips of her sex open. He blew lightly against her skin. "Fuck. Seriously. You are beautiful here. Your skin is bright pink and I can see your juices glistening, beckoning me. You're wet for me, Mack. *Me*." Dax lowered his head and nuzzled against her inner thigh. Mackenzie heard him inhale loudly.

"And your smell. Fucking divine." One of his thumbs moved until it was rubbing against her bundle of nerves.

"Oh my God, Daxton. What are you...yeah...right there."

"Here, Mack? Right here?" Dax pushed down harder and laughed as she squirmed under him. He eased a finger on his other hand into her tight sheath. "Or here?"

"Daxton!" Mackenzie couldn't get any other words out. She inhaled as Daxton's finger brushed against something inside that sent shockwaves shooting up through her body. "Oh my God."

"Yeah, Mack. That's it. Relax, feel it. Just enjoy my touch." Dax continued, taking his time, learning Mackenzie's body. He let her get used to him, his touch. He'd stroke her clit, then move his hand and caress her inner thigh. He used his mouth to suck and lick. Mackenzie writhed on the bed beneath him and Dax had never felt so masculine. He hadn't been completely sure he'd be able to make her come; hell, she knew her body better than he did, but he'd hoped. Now, running his hands and tongue over her folds, he knew she was on the verge of a monster orgasm.

Dax eased his finger back inside her sheath, loving how hot and wet she was. He curled his finger and brushed against the front wall of her body, stroking and fingering the bundle of nerves inside her body.

"Daxton...I—"

"That's it, baby. That's it. Let it happen. Right there...just a little more."

Mackenzie wasn't hearing Daxton anymore. All she heard was a ringing in her ears. She pushed her hips up and down, jerking in Daxton's grasp. She had no control over her own body. Mackenzie didn't even realize when her hands came down from over her head and grasped Daxton's shoulders hard enough to leave ten little indentations with her fingernails.

Just when Mackenzie didn't think she was going to make it over the edge, Daxton lowered his head and sucked her clit into his mouth as his free hand went up and pinched her nipple tightly. She'd never had a man handle her as roughly as Dax was, but the slight pain, combined with the fast flicking of his tongue on her clit and his finger thrusting in and out of her body, was all it took.

"Oh my God, Daxton! I'm coming!" Mackenzie gasped in disbelief. She threw her head back and whimpered as her first orgasm at a man's hand coursed through her body. She thrust up again and again, clenching on Dax's finger as she went over the edge. It seemed to last forever and Mackenzie couldn't stop her body from shuddering with aftershocks as Daxton removed his hand and stroked her body lightly.

When Mackenzie came back to herself, she found Daxton's face right next to hers. He'd pulled himself up and was resting his head on his right hand and his left was running up and down her body, stroking and caressing as he went.

"Welcome back."

Mackenzie could feel herself blushing. "Hi."

"Forgive me if I'm remembering wrong, but I thought you said you weren't good at this sex thing." Dax smiled as he said it.

Mackenzie moved her hand and stroked over Daxton's belly, caressing his hard abs, much as he was doing to her own body. "That's the first time... thefirsttimeamanhasmademecome." Her words were said quickly so they all bunched together. Then she continued in a more normal voice, not giving Dax time to say anything. "I know, it's ridiculous, right? I'm thirty-seven years old, you'd think at some point in the last, oh, twenty years or so someone would've gotten lucky and done just the right thing, touched just the right spot at the right time, but it never happened. Don't get me wrong, I've gotten myself off while I've...uh...you know, but a guy...all on his own? No. I've never had an orgasm with a guy where I didn't have to help."

Dax leaned in and whispered in her ear a bit cockily, "It won't be the last."

Mackenzie smiled up at him. "Can I touch you?"

"Nothing would please me more, sweetheart." Dax rolled over until he was on his back and put his hands behind his head as if he was lying down for a nap. Mackenzie sat up, got on her knees next to him, and looked down in awe.

"Whoa, Daxton. I know I've seen this before, but hiding this under your uniform has to be a crime. You really do have a fucking fourteen-pack. When I try to keep you from getting up to work out, just ignore me, will ya?"

Daxton chuckled. "Glad you approve, sweetheart."

"Oh, I approve all right."

Mackenzie ran her eyes up and down his body, stopping at his shoulders. She ran a finger over the small puncture wounds on the tops of his shoulders. "Did I do that?"

Dax moved one hand from under his head and caught Mackenzie's hand in his. He brought it up to his mouth and kissed her palm, running his tongue over the long line after kissing it. "Yeah, and it felt awesome. Remember when I talked about erotic pain? Yeah, I wasn't feeling anything. I was too busy enjoying the hell out of watching you come."

He put his hand back under his head and lifted his chin to her. "Go on, make yourself at home."

Mackenzie did what Daxton asked. She started by leaning over and licking each of the ten little wounds she'd put in his skin with her nails. Then she moved her head lower and sucked on Daxton's nipples, while running her hands up and down his body. Slowly, enjoying the feel of his stomach muscles jerking under her ministrations, Mack shifted to his erection. He was long and thick, and Mackenzie could see fluid shining on the head.

Maneuvering between his legs, and grunting in approval when he widened his stance so she could kneel between them, Mackenzie gripped his balls with one hand and used the other to caress his shaft. She spread his wetness over her palm, making it easier to glide up and down.

Not able to stop herself, Mackenzie leaned over and licked the head of his shaft so she could taste him. She looked up from between Daxton's legs to see him staring down at her with an intense look on his face.

"I want to be inside you, Mack. I can't wait much longer."

"But I'm just getting started," Mackenzie pouted.

"Oh, you'll have your chance, it just isn't right now."

"Condom?"

Dax indicated with his head to the table next to the bed. "There."

Mackenzie had to let go of Daxton and crawl up to where he'd gestured. When she leaned over him, Daxton guided her nipple into his mouth with a hand and sucked hard, making Mackenzie whimper in need.

"Let go, Daxton. I need you too."

Dax let go of Mack's breast with a small popping sound and allowed her to reach forward for the condom on the side table.

She eased back with the packet in her hand.

"Put it on me," Dax growled.

Mackenzie nodded and without losing eye contact, she put the packet up to her mouth and ripped it open with her teeth. She finally had to look down so she could see what she was doing. She pinched the tip, eased the condom over Daxton's erection, and smoothed it into place.

Before Mackenzie could think about what to do next, Daxton had her flipped over and she was on her back looking up at him. He paused above her, not saying anything, not moving, just watching her intently.

"Please, Daxton." Mack tried desperately to pull him down to her, to rub against him. She wanted him inside. Now.

He moved slowly, taking himself in his hand and pressing against her wet heat, easing himself into her tight sheath inch by inch. He didn't stop until he was all the way inside, then he lowered down until they were touching from toes to chest. "Perfect."

Mackenzie closed her eyes briefly against the small bite of pain she'd felt as Daxton entered her. It'd been a while and her body needed to adjust to having a man inside again. When the pain faded, she opened her eyes and held on tightly to Daxton's biceps as he slowly withdrew from her body, then pushed back in. He held her eyes the entire time. He slowly increased his speed as he moved in and out of Mack's body.

"You feel good, Daxton. I love how you fill me up. Faster. Go faster."

"You'll take it how I give it, Mack. You like this?"

"Yeah."

"You're hot and slick around me. I can feel your heat through the condom. As much as I love how you feel, I can't wait to get inside you without anything between us. Ah...you like that, don't you? I could feel you clench around me."

"Yeah, I want to feel you. Just you."

"You'll get me, babe. I'll pump you so full, as soon as I pull away from your tight body, our juices will leak out. When I take you standing up, you'll feel us dripping down your leg."

"Oh God, Daxton. That's so uh...realistic and slightly gross, but honestly, I can't wait."

Dax sped up his thrusts until he was pounding into her.

Mackenzie watched as Daxton closed his eyes and his muscles tightened. He was on the verge of losing it. "Yeah, that's it, Daxton, come for me. Don't wait for me. I want to watch you come." Mack tightened her inner muscles as hard as she could, squeezing him from the inside out. "Do it. Fuck me. You feel so good."

At her words, Dax couldn't hold back anymore. He reached down and pulled up Mackenzie's thighs until he could hook his elbows under her knees. "Hold on, Mack. Let me know if I hurt you."

"You won't hurt me, Daxton. Do it. I love when you pound into me. The friction of your skin against mine feels awesome."

Dax let go of his iron control, using Mack's permission to fuck her like he'd dreamed of for so long. He hammered into her, and when he felt Mackenzie pinch his nipples, he couldn't hold his orgasm in any longer. He ground into her, holding himself inside as tightly as he could and let go. His hips undulated against her once, twice, and then three times. He groaned loud and long.

Finally, feeling empty, he eased down next to Mack, holding her to him so he didn't slip out. He hiked her leg up over his lap, keeping their connection intact. "Holy shit. You killed me."

Mackenzie giggled, and Dax loved the sound. "I think that was my line."

"Nope, definitely mine." Dax picked up his head and looked Mackenzie in the eyes. "Just so you know. I'm going to make it my mission in life to make you come with me."

"Daxton, I told you—"

Dax put his finger over Mack's lips to stop her words. "Shhh, I know what you said, and I don't believe it for a second. Anyone who came as hard as you did with just my finger and the brief touch of my mouth to your clit…can orgasm with penetration. We just need to keep practicing. And I'll enjoy the hell out of that practice in the meantime."

"You're crazy. We're too old for this shit."

"No, we're not. I don't feel too old and I'm nine years older than you. So if I can do it, you can too."

"Whatever." Mackenzie's words were muffled against his chest.

"Let me take care of this condom, and we can get some sleep."

Mackenzie watched as Daxton rolled away from her and went into the bathroom. He came out not long after.

"You need to use the bathroom?"

"No, I think I'm good."

"Okay, lift up so I can get you under the sheet."

Mackenzie lifted up one butt cheek enough so Daxton could pull the sheet out from under her. He climbed in next to her and hauled her into his arms.

"You don't have to—"

"Shut it. I want to. I'll go absolutely insane if I can't hold you in my arms."

Mackenzie didn't say a word, but dipped her chin and fit her head under Daxton's chin. She put her arm around his chest. One leg came up and wrapped itself around his thigh.

"Comfy?"

Mackenzie could hear the laughter in Daxton's voice, but didn't care.

"Yeah, extremely."

"Go to sleep, sweetheart."

"I don't have to get up early tomorrow, do I? It's Saturday. It's against my religion to get out of bed before nine on the weekend."

"You don't have to get up early, Mack. Just sleep."

"Okay. Thank you for making this easy and not weird."

"You're welcome."

Mackenzie fell asleep almost immediately. Dax stayed awake a bit longer, enjoying the soft breaths Mack made as she slept and wondering how in the hell he'd gotten so lucky.

CHAPTER 10

TWO WEEKS after Mackenzie had spent the night for the first time, Dax knew for sure she was the woman for him. They'd settled into a regular routine. They'd leave together each morning for work, and over the course of the day figure out whose place they'd spend the night at, then they'd meet there after work. They'd make or go out for dinner, then head to bed, making the most of their time together.

Dax had several sets of uniforms over at Mackenzie's apartment, just as she had plenty of work clothes to choose from at his. Not one night had gone by that they hadn't spent together, and Dax couldn't be happier.

Mackenzie was just as cute now as Dax had thought she was on their first date, perhaps more so.

She was who she was and didn't have a devious bone in her body…something that was refreshing to Dax.

The day Mackenzie met TJ again was one of Dax's favorite memories. He'd taken Mack out to dinner, knowing TJ was going to meet them there. TJ slid into the booth across from them and Dax laughed until his stomach hurt at the look on Mack's face. She'd blushed a fiery red and stammered a bit before getting her wits about her.

"Daxton Chambers, I can't believe you didn't tell me Officer Rockwell would be here tonight!"

"TJ, babe. Call me TJ."

"TJ then. Am I allowed to thank you for not giving me a ticket? Or is that bad cop karma and I'll end up getting six tickets in the next month as a result?"

TJ and Dax laughed. "You're welcome, and as long as you don't decide to be a speed demon or start stealing from the neighborhood grocery store, I think you're good."

"So does that mean I can drop your name—yours too, Daxton—and I can get out of any tickets in the future?"

"Mack, how many times had you been stopped before we pulled you over? Or since? I don't think you have anything to worry about. You usually drive like an old granny," Dax said, picking on Mackenzie.

"Shut up. Maybe I'll take up street racing now that my boyfriend is a Texas Ranger and I know not only an SAPD Officer, but a Highway Patrolman too!"

"I don't think so, sweetheart. If you get stopped you'll have to take your chances just like everyone else."

"Don't you guys have like some secret sticker I can put on my car that's like a 'get-out-of-a-ticket-free' card?"

"Sorry, Mackenzie, there's no such thing." TJ was smiling broadly, resting his elbows on the table.

"Well, poo. There should be one. I should get *something* out of dating a police officer!"

That night, Dax had reminded Mack what she was getting out of dating a police officer...him. He'd brought her to the edge of orgasm several times, pulling back right before she'd been about to explode. He'd gotten his test results back from the doctor the day before, and Dax couldn't tease her for long before he had to be inside her. Having pity on her, he'd finally pushed her over the edge, loving how she shuddered and shook in his arms.

After she'd come apart, Dax had hauled her out of the bed and pushed her face down, leaning over the mattress. He'd taken her from behind as she moaned and thrashed on the covers. While she'd technically done it doggy style before, that had been completely different. They'd snuggled together afterwards and Dax didn't think either one of them had moved a muscle all night.

Dax looked over at Mack standing in his kitchen. It was Friday morning and they were about ready to head to work. Mackenzie was leaning on the counter in front of his toaster, gazing at the bagel within as if it would cook faster if she glared it into submission while it cooked.

Dax walked up behind her and pulled her into the front of his body.

"I'm on call this weekend again."

Mackenzie turned and put her arms around him as far as they'd go. "Okay. You want me to stay here, or are you coming to my place?"

Dax shook his head, loving how Mack didn't give him any grief for having to work on the weekend. Kelly had hated if he had an overnight shift when he'd worked at the El Paso Police Department, and had made his life miserable every time he came home from those shifts.

"Whatever you want, Mack."

She thought about it for a second, then finally said, "Okay, my place. I'll make dinner and put it in the fridge and if you're hungry when you get home, you can eat. You have clothes over there?"

"Yeah, I'm good."

"Okay then."

"Okay then."

"Just so you know, in case you were wondering. Sleeping alone, waiting for you to get home, sucks. I'm not complaining, just saying…I've gotten used to your warm body next to mine and I actually feel cold in my bed until you get home. I've never felt that way before. I even contemplated putting on a T-shirt the last time you worked late."

"You better not put anything on. I like you naked and waiting when I get to you."

"What if someone breaks in?"

"No one is breaking in. Make sure the doors are locked and you'll be fine."

Mackenzie smiled at Daxton. The first thing he'd done after the first time he'd spent the night was go to the hardware store and buy new locks to upgrade what she already had. She hadn't minded; she'd always rather be safe than sorry.

"Okay, Daxton. Can I ask you something?"

"Of course."

Mackenzie ignored the ding of the toaster indicating her bagel was ready and soldiered on. "I know you can't talk about your cases, but I worry about you. I know the crap you have to do sucks, and I don't want you to think I'm some wilting wallflower who can't take hearing some tough stuff from you every now and then. If you need to talk about a case or something that happened, I'm here for you. I think we're past the get-to-know-you stage where all we talk about is hearts and flowers."

"Hearts and flowers?" Dax smiled at Mack, she was so fucking adorable. He thought that about her about a thousand times a day.

"Yeah, hearts and fucking flowers. You know how I feel about my boss. She's a bitch. She doesn't care about anyone in the office and makes us do work over, just because she can. The other day she actually complained that I'd found a mistake in one of the spreadsheets she'd already checked over. She'd prefer the work she did be wrong, just so she didn't 'look bad' in front of her bosses. It's ridiculous. And you know about Mark and Matthew and how they drive me crazy. You know a million other things about me that aren't things people who are trying to impress each other know. I just want you to know you can share right back."

Dax turned with Mack in his arms and pulled her up until she was sitting on the island in the middle of the kitchen and they were face-to-face. He stepped into her and she spread her legs so he was right up in her space. He hauled her hips to the edge of the counter and held her against him. "I know I can share with you, Mack. I haven't done it, not because I don't trust you, or because I'm trying to hide anything...okay, that might be a lie. I don't *want* to tell you some of the shit I see and hear in my job because I like you just the way you are. You have a unique take on life and I don't want to see your light dim because of the shit that happens in my world. I like that you're naïve about the seedier side of life and my job."

"But you need to talk about it."

"And I do. I talk with Quint, and Cruz, and TJ, and other very good men and women who are in law enforcement. We have lunch together. We go to conferences together. We see each other in the field and in task-force meetings. I promise you, sweetheart, I'm not holding shit in that will make me lose it. I'm forty-six years old and have been in this job for a hell of a long time. If I hadn't learned to deal before now, I'd have had a heart attack. Okay?"

Dax watched as Mackenzie processed what he'd just told her. He loved that she never agreed with him just to shut him up. She'd been known to argue with him about something for hours on end, if she truly believed what she said or thought was the right way.

Mackenzie brought her hands up to the back of Daxton's neck and laced her fingers together. "Okay,

I believe you. I don't know what's normal for a cop's girlfriend to know and not know. I'd never want you to think I wasn't interested in what you did for a living."

"I know it, sweetheart. Swear."

"Good. I have something else to tell you, since we're having this deep chat and all."

Dax smiled. "What's that?"

"Sunday we're going over to my mom's for lunch. I hope that's okay. She understands that you had to cancel both times we tried to arrange it before, after I told her you were a big bad Texas Ranger and you had to save the world. But mom's decided it's time. Hell, they decided it was time about a month ago, but they're not going to let us out of it for much longer. And to be honest, I'm glad we haven't been able to make it over there yet, I've been trying to make you so infatuated with me that no matter what they throw at you, you'll ignore it and not break up with me."

"Do they have any bodies buried in their backyards?"

"Daxton!"

Ignoring Mack's tone of outrage and smiling as he continued, Dax said, "No? Then relax, Mack. I know how families are. It'll be fine. You certainly don't have to try any harder to make me infatuated with you. I'm already there."

Ignoring his words that made her insides flutter, Mackenzie retorted, "Well, I appreciate that, however you haven't actually met my family yet and I don't want you to decide after tonight that I'm a loon and rather than deal with my crazy family after breaking up with me, you change your name and move out of the state."

Daxton laughed, and she told him she was only half-way kidding, "Daxton, you have no clue. I'm the only girl in our family. Now that dad's gone, Mark and Matthew won't care that you're forty-six and I'm in my upper thirties. They'll probably take you out back for a birds-and-the-bees chat. And mom will probably have the pastor there and he'll be ready to perform a wedding ceremony over tea and crackers. You have no idea how insane they are. I just wanted to warn you ahead of time."

Dax leaned in and moved one of his hands from Mackenzie's hip to her back and up to her neck. He held her still in his arms by tightening his hold. In a low, serious voice, without a trace of humor, he told her, "I wouldn't be opposed to a wedding."

"Holy shit, you did not just say that." Mackenzie could feel her heart beating a million miles an hour, she curled her hands and unconsciously dug her blunt nails into Daxton's neck.

"I said it. I'm not proposing, Mack. Not right now. But I sure as hell can see you in my future. I like you in my life, in my bed, in my space. I like it a lot. You're cute as all get out, we're more than matched in bed, and we're practically living together already. I'll meet your family this weekend, they'll like me, and I'll like them. I'm not sure either of us is ready for 'I love yous' yet, but it's coming, sweetheart."

"Daxton."

Dax waited for Mack to say something. When she didn't, he smiled at her. "Mackenzie."

"I...dammit. I don't want to go to my job and deal with the bitchface I work for. I don't want you to go and talk to scumsuckers. I want to barricade us in your room, get naked, and not leave for the rest of our lives."

"I think we'd get hungry eventually."

Mack smiled, glad the extreme-emotion sharing seemed to be over. "And stinky."

"And we'd eventually get kicked out because we couldn't pay the rent."

"And my family would come over wondering where we were."

"I'll miss you tonight, sweetheart. Stay safe for me. I'll come to you as soon as I can."

It looked as though the emotional part of the morning wasn't quite over yet. "I always miss you too, Daxton."

"Okay, I'm going then. I'll see you tonight. I have a new position I want us to try. I think you'll like it. I read about it in a book once and I think you're flexible enough. Sunday we'll go to your mom's house. Text me today and let me know how your day is going."

Shivering at the lustful look in his eyes, Mackenzie said simply, "I will. Bye, Daxton."

"Bye, Mack."

Dax kissed Mackenzie swiftly, knowing if he lingered, he might just get carried away and lock them in his bedroom as she suggested. He backed away, headed away from the temptation she offered, and out the front door.

Mackenzie hopped down off the counter, not smiling, and headed for the toaster. If she wasn't mistaken, Daxton had just told her he loved her...not in so many words, but he might as well have.

Finally, she smiled to herself as she dug the cream cheese out of the fridge. Daxton loved her. Holy shit. It was gonna be a good day.

* * *

Dax rolled his head and tried to work the kinks out of his neck. His morning chat with Mack notwithstanding, his day had not started out well. He'd arrived at work to find three letters addressed to him sitting on his desk with a note from the administrative assistant. She'd apologized and said the letters had been delayed in getting to him. She'd been on vacation for a week and a half and no one had bothered to hand the mail out to the appropriate Rangers in her absence.

He'd opened the first, and dropped it immediately seeing who had sent it. Dax had leaned over his desk, being careful not to touch the paper any more than he already had, read the extremely alarming words, and called the Major. It was from the Lone Star Reaper. This time the letter was addressed specifically to Dax. The thought didn't give him warm-fuzzies. While Dax didn't know if the other two letters were from the Reaper, he wasn't taking any chances.

Three hours later, he'd received a call from Quint and had been asked to come to a joint task-force meeting. Knowing he wouldn't like what he was about to find out, Dax braced himself.

The meeting included the Chief of Police at the

SAPD, Quint, Cruz, the Major from his Ranger Company and a few other high-ranking officers.

"Dax, thanks for coming, and thanks for the quick response with those letters. They're being worked over now and preliminary thoughts are that we might have a partial print on one of them this time," the Major said.

"So all three were from the Reaper?" Dax asked.

"Yeah."

Silence fell over the room and Dax knew they weren't telling him something important. "What did the other letters say? Did he give the locations of more victims?"

"Yeah, we have three separate teams checking out the cemeteries he mentioned in the notes."

"Why did he change his M.O. now?" Dax wondered out loud. "He used to call in the body locations, but now he's writing me a letter like he's my fucking pen pal?"

"The Reaper is escalating his game and changed the rules in the middle," The Chief of Police said unnecessarily.

"Yeah," Dax agreed in a tight voice. "He's made it way more personal now. He sent these notes specifically to me," Dax said, stating the obvious.

Cruz ran his hand over his face, then up and over his short-cropped black hair. "It's more serious than that." Cruz shuffled through the piles of various reports and evidence sitting in front of him and handed over three sheets of photocopied paper. "I'm sorry, Dax."

Dax clenched his teeth. Fuck. He pulled the copies toward him and read the notes the Reaper had left. He'd already read the first one, but the others were just as horrifying.

DAXTON CHAMBERS, you might be a tough ol Ranger, but id like to see you catch me. You can find a present ive left you in Johnson cemetery. I thnk youll find her to your liking. 5'4, curvy and brunette. Sounds like just your type.

So, you decided to ignore my last letter. Fine. Maybe you wont ignore this one. Check out my latest beauty in White Oak cemetery. She fought valiantly, but in the end she succumbed just like all the others. I nicknamed her M&M.

THE LAST NOTE was the most chilling.

FUCK YOU CHAMBERS. You think im joking? You think

shes safe? Shes not. I hope youre enjoying fucking your new girlfriend. No one is safe from the Reaper. Do you know where Mackenzie is right this second? I wonder how long shed last in one of my coffins. Im sure shell be my favorite yet. Ive got big plans for your little cutie. In the meantime check Shadows End cemetery to see how that Mackenzie fared.

DAX STOOD up so abruptly the chair he'd been sitting in fell backward with a crash. He stalked over to the side of the room and punched the wall. Ignoring the pain in his fist, he leaned over, grabbed the windowsill with both hands, and panted, trying to control the need to beat the shit out of someone.

The fucker knew about Mackenzie. Had threatened her. Was choosing women who looked like Mack, who were even *named* Mackenzie. Dax felt sick. Knowing he was going to lose his breakfast, he strode over the trashcan in the corner of the room and threw up. He stayed crouched in front of the plastic container, hands on his thighs, using everything he'd learned in his training to regulate his breathing and get his equilibrium back.

He was a Texas Ranger. He didn't act like this. Then again, the woman he loved hadn't ever been threatened and targeted by a psychotic serial killer either.

He loved Mack. He'd been pretty sure of his feelings before, but thinking of this psycho getting his hands on her solidified it.

"When were the letters sent?" Dax's voice was low and brittle. He was proud his voice only cracked once. He stood up, and wiped his face on his sleeve and faced the other officers in the room, not embarrassed in the least by his break in control. He knew they all understood. He stalked over, grabbed a bottled water off of the conference table, and chugged half of it waiting on Quint's response.

"The last one was postmarked five days ago."

"Jesus fucking Christ." Dax said the words under his breath and pulled out his phone. He had to get ahold of Mack now. He couldn't wait for the meeting to be over. He had to reassure himself that she was at work and fine. He looked down and wanted to cry at the silly little texts she'd left him over the last couple of hours.

CAN *we rewind and make a different decision? Bitchface is being extra bitchy today.*

. . .

Is it too late for me to join up and become a cop?

Are you sure there are no secret stickers that will get me out of jail free?

I just wanted to let you know I was thinking about you. Miss you.

Dax hit Mackenzie's name and brought the phone up to his ear, waiting for her to pick up. He turned his back to the room and stood next to the wall looking down at his feet.

"Hey Daxton! What's up?"

"I just wanted to call and see how you were doing."

"I'm good, except for you-know-who. But that's nothing new."

"Change of plans tonight, sweetheart."

"Yeah?"

Dax knew the way Mackenzie stretched out the word, she was thinking sexy thoughts, but he couldn't bring himself to banter with her as he usually would.

"Yeah, I still have to work late, but TJ is gonna

pick you up from work and take you back to my place. He'll stay there with you until I get home." Dax hadn't asked TJ, but he knew he'd protect Mackenzie until Dax could get home, no questions asked.

"Is everything okay?" Mackenzie's voice was serious, and no longer teasing. She'd obviously picked up on the fact that something was seriously wrong.

"No. But it will be. Trust me, sweetheart. Okay?"

"With my life, Daxton. What about my car?"

"Leave it. It'll be fine. If we need to move it later, I'll get one of the other Rangers to help me out with it."

"Are you all right?"

Dax lowered his voice. "I'm okay, Mack."

"Swear?"

"I'm okay."

"You didn't swear."

"Mackenzie—"

"Okay. I'll stop. Just...be safe all right? I can't lose you."

"You aren't losing me." Dax didn't know what else to say to reassure her. He knew she was freaked out. She wasn't rambling on and on as she usually did. Dax knew it was his fault. "There's some shit going on at work, and unfortunately there could be some blowback on you and me. We've got it under control, but in the meantime I need you to be smart and safe. Okay, Mack? Don't be one of those 'too stupid to live' women you bitch about in those romances you read. Be safe. Be alert. Don't leave work for lunch or on breaks. Wait in your office for TJ to come inside for you. All right? Can you do that for me?"

"Yes." Mackenzie's answer was immediate and strong. "Blowback?"

"I'll explain tonight."

"All right, Daxton. I...fuck...okay here goes. Ready? Iloveyou." Her words were fast and jumbled together. "I've only loved one other boyfriend before in my life and that was when I was eight years old. He'd chase me around the playground, corner me, and kiss me. Then he'd run away again. He brought me bubble gum as presents and even let me have the Little Debbie oatmeal cream pie from his lunch one day. I told him I loved him and he freaked out. He never chased me again and made it a point to sit on the other side of the lunchroom after that. He moved away the next year and I never saw him again, but I've never told any guy that I've loved him since then.

"I don't know what's going on, but I want to make sure I tell you now. I'd hate for something to happen and not be able to tell you. Okay? You don't have to say it back, because I know you're stressed, I can hear it in your voice, and you're probably surrounded by a hundred other cops and shit and they're probably staring at you and you can't say anything anyway, cos it'd make you look like a wuss. So it's okay, but *you* stay safe. Don't do anything crazy, wear your bulletproof vest, even though it's hot and you don't like how you can't move that well with it on. I'll wait for TJ and won't do anything stupid. I swear."

Dax closed his eyes. Fuck, he loved this woman. How the hell she'd managed to make him smile when there was abso-fucking-lutely *nothing* to smile about was beyond him. "I love you too, Mack."

"You said it." Her words were whispered. "Are you alone?"

"Nope." Dax turned around and looked at the men around the table, all of whom were watching him curiously. None were hiding their eavesdropping. "There are about eight guys from four different agencies sitting here staring at me."

"Daxton—"

"I gotta go, sweetheart."

"Okay." Mackenzie was still whispering.

"I'll still be late tonight, but I'll be home. There's an extra T-shirt in my top drawer."

Dax smiled as Mack chuckled. "Guess I'm not sleeping naked tonight?"

"Not while TJ is there."

"Okay, Daxton. Love you. Be safe."

"Love you too. See you later. Bye." The words felt natural and right.

Dax clicked off the phone and shoved it back into his pocket. He strode to the table and grabbed his chair, setting it back on its feet. Sitting down, he looked around the room and asked gruffly, "What the hell are we doing to catch this asshole?"

The men around the table began strategizing. No way in hell would they allow the Reaper to get ahold of Dax's woman. She was one of them now. Period.

CHAPTER 11

MACKENZIE LAY IN BED WIDE-AWAKE. TJ had arrived to pick her up with about fifteen minutes left to go in the workday. He hadn't said much, just sat in her office waiting for her to be done. Mackenzie hastily finished up and didn't put up a fuss at all when TJ put his arm around her waist as he guided her to his patrol car.

It was obvious there was something terribly wrong, and Mackenzie didn't know what to do or say, so she did as TJ asked, and moved beside him without hesitation to his car. When they'd arrived at Daxton's apartment, TJ didn't waste any time, but guided her to the door, telling her to wait just inside the apartment as he entered and made sure it was clear before allowing her inside.

Mackenzie made spaghetti for dinner. It was

quick and easy. TJ thanked her and they ate in relative silence. She really *really* wanted to know what was going on, but Mackenzie figured TJ probably wouldn't tell her.

They watched some silly reality show set in Australia with lots of extremely catty and bitchy women all fighting for the man to pass the time. Mackenzie had asked once if they could turn it to the news, and when TJ had refused, she knew whatever was happening was probably being talked about on the local news stations. She let it drop; preferring to hear what it was straight from Daxton.

Around nine o'clock, Mackenzie told TJ she was going to bed. He didn't say anything other than, "Sleep well." As if.

Mackenzie put on one of Daxton's Ranger T-shirts, as he'd requested, knowing she probably wouldn't be able to sleep nude again until whatever was happening was over, and huddled under the comforter waiting for Daxton to get home. She turned on her side and hugged the pillow he usually used to her chest, burying her nose into it, inhaling Daxton's comforting smell.

Two hours later, Mackenzie was still wide-awake, jumping at every sound she heard outside, when she heard TJ and Daxton talking to one another in the other room. She didn't move. She lay still, waiting for Daxton to come to her.

Mackenzie watched as the bedroom door opened quietly and saw Daxton enter the room. He didn't hesitate, but came straight to the bed as if he knew she wouldn't be asleep. He laid himself out on top of the covers and pulled Mackenzie into his arms, pillow and all.

Dax wrapped his arms around Mack with one hand at her nape and the other around her waist. He dipped his head and snuggled his nose into the crook of her neck. He sighed when he felt her arms snake up between them to come to rest around his shoulders. They were as close as they could be, and still be fully clothed.

"I'm sorry, Mack."

"Don't."

"But—"

"No. This isn't your fault. I don't know whose fault it is yet, but I know it's not yours. So don't apologize for something someone else is doing to us…whatever it is they're doing."

"If I wasn't a Ranger—"

Mackenzie lifted her head and tried to squint in the darkness at him. "Seriously, Daxton. Stop it. You *are* a Ranger. You're a fucking awesome Ranger. I love you because of the man you are. If you weren't a

Ranger, we might not be together. I don't know what's going on yet, but the way I choose to look at it is that you've worked your entire life to get to this point. You've learned what you needed to learn, you know what you need to know to stop whatever it is. I believe in you. I love you."

"Fuck, sweetheart." Dax didn't say anything else, just held the most important thing in his life tightly in his arms. "I love you too." Dax's words were soft and heartfelt.

Mackenzie pulled back. "Did TJ go?"

"Yeah."

She pushed at Daxton. "Are you hungry?"

"No."

"All right. Go get ready for bed, I'll be right here waiting. You can tell me whatever you can or need to when you get back."

Dax took a deep breath, inhaling the unique smell that Mack always seemed to carry with her. It was sweet. Some sort of sugar smell. Vanilla? He didn't know, but he loved how it mixed with the natural essence of her skin. He forced himself to loosen his arms and roll out of bed. He quickly got ready in the bathroom and stripped off his pants and shirt on the way back to bed.

Dax left on his boxers for the first time since they'd started sleeping together. He'd noticed Mack had on his shirt, as he'd requested, but figured she felt as vulnerable as he did being completely nude... and she didn't even know what was going on.

He climbed under the covers and pulled the pillow out of Mack's arms. He turned her on her back and propped himself up next to her with his head resting on one hand and the other on her belly under the shirt she was wearing. He didn't beat around the bush.

"The Lone Star Reaper struck again. Three more bodies were found today."

"Oh, Daxton. That sucks."

"Yeah. He sent the notes to me, telling me where to find them."

"What?"

Dax continued, wanting to get the worst over with so they could talk through what their next steps were.

"He sent the notes to me personally. He inferred that he's been watching me. He knows about you, Mack. He mentioned you specifically in the notes, by name."

"Oh my God."

"It gets worse. Can you handle it, or do you want to wait until later?"

"Worse?" Mackenzie's voice was soft. Dax heard

her take a deep breath. "I can handle it. Tell it all to me now, we'll deal together."

"His last two victims looked like you, and the last woman was named Mackenzie." Dax didn't pause to let her process his words, he kept going. "He fucked up though, Mack. We got prints this time. We're going to get him. He won't touch you." Dax knew he was stretching the truth a bit. Even with this guy's prints, if he hadn't been arrested and his prints weren't in the system, they wouldn't do any good, but he'd say just about anything right now to reassure Mack.

"O-o-okay, Daxton. Okay."

"You've got to be vigilant though, sweetheart. I'm afraid going to your mom's on Sunday is out. I don't know if he knows about your family, but I'd rather not involve them right now, or have us go there and have him somehow use them against you. I'd love for you to stay home from work for a while, but I don't know if that will be possible. If not, okay, but you'll have to do some basic things for me. Can you do that?"

"I can't stay home. There are like, three big projects coming up due. Nancy would flip her shit if I wasn't there to do them for her and for her to take credit for them."

"All right, can you listen to what I want you to do to stay safe then?"

"Of course. I don't want to be buried alive, Daxton. I'll do whatever you tell me to."

Dax stopped long enough to lean over and kiss the side of Mackenzie's head, then he leaned back. "I'll drop you off at work each morning, and either one of the guys or I will pick you up each night. I know you've only met TJ and Quint, but I swear to you that you can trust Cruz, Conor, and Hayden, and even the other Rangers, as much as you do me. I'll be sure to introduce you so you'll feel more comfortable around them. Don't leave the office, not even for a quick errand. That's going to be a pain in the ass, I know it, but it's important. I don't want him snatching you when you're in the grocery store or something."

"No problem. I can do that."

"You'll never be home alone. I want you to stay here. My place is more secure than yours. I'm assuming he knows where I live, but he definitely knows about you. We need to come up with a plan in case he does something crazy like set a fire or something."

"Set a fire? Holy shit. Daxton—"

"Yeah, I know, stay with me, baby..." Dax could

feel how freaked Mack was because she was gripping his biceps so hard, he knew she'd leave marks.

"Okay. Okay, go on."

"If something happens and we have to leave the apartment because of a crisis, don't panic. Stick close to me, or whoever I have here to watch over you. Don't leave my side. If someone calls you and says I'm hurt or killed or whatever, do *not* rush off on your own. It'd be a ploy to get you away from whatever protection you've got. You text me every hour and let me know you're okay; even if I don't answer, know that I'm watching and waiting for your text."

"I'm scared. No, I'm fucking petrified."

"I know, and I'm so sorry. Do you know what I did when I first read the notes he'd sent me, threatening you?"

"What?"

"I threw up. Literally. I puked my guts out in front of a room full of cops. I'm scared for both of us, sweetheart."

"Oh, Daxton." Mackenzie took a deep breath. She had to get herself together. It was obvious Daxton had thought a lot about how to keep her safe, and he'd gone to great lengths to arrange everything. "I swear I won't be stupid. You said you got his prints. Why can't you just go pick him up if you know who it is?"

"Forensics doesn't work in real life like it does on television. It doesn't take an hour or two to get results back, unfortunately. It can take weeks. This case is taking precedence, so hopefully it won't take that long, but we have to wait. Fingerprints don't typically take as long as DNA samples, but the bad thing is that his prints might not be in the system. If he's never been arrested or had his prints taken for a job and put in the database, we won't know who he is."

"How long do you think this will go on?"

"I don't know, Mack. I simply don't know."

"Should I leave town? I mean, I can go on an extended vacation somewhere. Or something. I know I said I needed to be at work, but fuck it. I'd rather lose my job and be alive than get caught by this guy."

"I love you, Mack. I love that you're completely practical and haven't thrown a hissy fit over your job or having been thrown a curve ball. The man in me wants to agree and to ship you off to some far-flung, out-of-the-way cabin in the woods where you can be safe, but the Ranger inside knows that probably wouldn't help. This guy is crazy. He could just follow you and get ahold of you wherever you went. I'd rather you be here, with me, so I can keep you safe, than to send you off by yourself where he might be able to track you. Besides, it gives me a chance to hold you in my arms every night."

"I'd rather be in your arms every night as well."

"Okay, so one more thing."

"Oh God, something else?" Mackenzie took a deep breath. "Sorry, sorry…okay, go ahead."

"Fuck." Dax's voice was low and tortured, but he plunged ahead. "We need a code word. Something that, if said, via text or over the phone, will alert us to the fact that something's wrong. How about if you say 'I'm so clumsy' to me, I'll know you're in trouble and I'll do everything in my power to get to you. If you hear me say, 'I'm busy,' you'll know something is wrong on my end and you need to hunker down and get to safety, no matter what getting to safety means. You know I'm never too busy for you, Mack, so if I say it, or text it, you'll know it's our code word. Yeah?"

"Yeah."

Dax dropped his head and put his forehead against Mackenzie's. "We're going to make it through this. I can't have met you after all these years, only to lose you now."

"Damn straight."

Dax smiled, even though he didn't really feel like it.

"You really puked in front of all your friends?"

179

"Yeah, Mack. I couldn't handle him threatening you and it made me physically sick to my stomach."

"I've never had someone throw up over me before. I mean, not because they were worried about me. I had a guy throw up *on* me before though. I was in college at a party and I was sitting next to this guy, minding my own business, and he didn't say anything just leaned over and, *buulllahh*, his dinner and most of the alcohol he'd drank in the last hour, was in my lap. Seriously, it was gross, and he didn't even know me. My brothers have been worried about me before. Once when I was on a trip with some friends to Amistad National Recreation Area west of San Antonio, the group decided they wanted to go to Cuidad Acuna to shop and my brothers about lost it. They were calling and texting me, but I'd turned my phone off, because, hello, I was in Mexico, and international rates are so expensive, and when I finally got back across the border I had to endure them yelling at me for hours...okay, well what seemed like hours. But no one, in my entire life, has been so worried about me that they actually threw up."

Dax took a breath to respond, but Mackenzie put her finger over his lips.

"As much as I like the sentiment behind you

losing your lunch, I don't like it. Don't do it again, Daxton."

Dax loved that, even freaked and scared, Mack could still lapse into her cute-as-hell ramblings when it'd really only take a sentence or two to say the same thing. "I can't say I liked it much either, sweetheart. But I'll tell you this. I'll always worry about you. Every moment you're not in my arms, I worry. I'll worry about a short trip to the store, or a simple walk to the mailboxes because I've seen too much shit in my life. I'll try to curb it, but you should know I'm going to be über-protective. Probably annoyingly so."

"You know what? Before today, I probably *would* have been annoyed. But not now. I know you have reasons to be. So I'll deal."

"I love you, Mack."

"I love you too."

"Whatever happens, know I'll do whatever I have to, to keep you safe."

"I know you will."

As the night lengthened, they held each other tight. Mackenzie finally fell asleep a couple hours later. Dax didn't sleep until the sky started brightening with the morning sun.

CHAPTER 12

MACKENZIE HAD a hard time concentrating on the spreadsheet in front of her. It'd been a long week and a half since the Lone Star Reaper had basically declared her his next victim. She'd spent most of that time scared to death, but trying not to show it. Daxton had enough stress on his plate, so she tried to hide her fears as much as she could. Mackenzie figured he knew she was scared, but was allowing her to have her delusion that she was hiding it from him.

He'd done just what he said he would. He'd dropped her off at work every morning and he, or one of his law enforcement friends, picked her up every day. Laine had freaked when Mackenzie had told her what had been going on. She'd met Daxton several times, but let Mack know in no uncertain terms how she felt about the fact that because of Dax's job, her friend had been targeted by a serial killer.

Mackenzie couldn't get pissed at Laine. If Laine had called Mack to tell her that her new boyfriend's job was dangerous and someone had threatened her life, Mack knew she'd be beyond worried about Laine as well. All Mack could do was try to reassure her friend that she was being careful and not taking any chances.

Mackenzie had watched the news...once. It was enough to wake her up in the middle of the night with a horrendous nightmare. She hadn't tried to watch it again and hadn't asked Daxton anything about the case since then either. Mackenzie knew he'd tell her if the threat was gone...or if it'd gotten worse.

The newscaster had droned on about the profile the FBI had done on the killer and warned the viewers to be careful and safe. Then they'd abruptly shown pictures of the latest victims. Three women; all short and overweight, all brown-haired. It was their names that had gotten to Mackenzie the most. The second woman's name was Monica Miller, first and last names starting with an M, just like hers. However, it was the last woman's name that sent chills down her body. Mackenzie McMillian.

It hadn't really hit home to Mack that she was the target of a serial killer until she'd seen those names on the screen, next to pictures of women who had the same body type and look as her; that she could actually be in extreme danger. She'd believed Daxton, but hearing him say it and seeing it were two completely different things.

After she'd woken up shaking and crying and completely freaked-out, Daxton had asked her not to watch the news unless he was either there with her, or until everything had played itself out. Mackenzie had no trouble agreeing immediately. Things were a bit too real for her right now and she didn't know if she ever wanted to watch the local news again.

Mackenzie picked up her phone and sent a short text to Daxton, letting him know all was well. She'd done just what he'd asked, to the letter. She hadn't been anywhere other than work and Daxton's apartment. When they'd needed groceries, Daxton had stopped on his way home from work one night. Mackenzie knew she should feel suffocated, but if she was honest with herself, she didn't.

The phone on her desk rang and Mackenzie picked it up after only one ring.

"Hello?"

"Hey, Mack, it's me."

"Hey, Daxton. How are you?" The simple phrase

had a whole new meaning now; one Mackenzie knew she'd never take for granted again.

"Good. Everything's good. You?"

"Same. No news?"

"No new news on the case, sorry. But I *do* have some news I think you'll like."

"I could use some good news, Daxton. Sock it to me."

"I'm getting off early today. Thought you might want to go on a mini-vacation with me."

"Yes."

"You don't know where we're going."

"I don't care where, as long as you're with me."

Dax's voice gentled. "Fuck, woman. How'd I get so lucky?"

"Where are you taking me, Daxton? Tahiti? Fiji? The Swiss Alps?"

"Nothing so grand, I'm afraid, but I'll put those on our bucket list. How about Austin?"

"Austin? What's in Austin?"

"I thought we'd take a long weekend and get out of here for a bit. I've reserved us a suite at Hotel Ella. It's a five-star hotel not far from the University of Texas campus. We can stay holed up all weekend and not have to worry about anything that's been going on."

"That sounds awesome, but if I'm going to be

able to take a day off, I have to get a lot of work done this afternoon. I'm not sure I'll be able to call or text you again…will that be okay?"

Dax thought about it for a moment, then agreed. "Okay, but don't leave your building. In fact, better yet, stay in your office all afternoon."

"But Dax," Mackenzie protested, "I can't sit here for another four hours! What if I have to use the bathroom? What if I get thirsty?"

"Don't leave your floor then. It's important, Mack."

"That I can do. I can't wait for the weekend. I've missed you."

"I know, sweetheart. I've missed you too. I want nothing more than to be able to put everything aside and concentrate on you again." Dax's voice turned teasing. "There are about three new positions I want to introduce you to, and some toys as well."

"Daxton! You can't say that stuff while I'm at work!"

"You love it."

"Maybe so, but still!"

Dax chuckled. "Okay, I'll be there to pick you up around five and we'll head straight up there."

"But I don't have any of my things with me."

"We'll stop at a store and grab some bathroom

stuff. You won't need any clothes, Mack. I plan on keeping you naked the entire weekend."

"Okay. I like that plan."

"I love you, Mack."

"Love you too. I'll see you in a few hours."

"Okay, babe. Bye."

"Bye."

Mackenzie hung up the phone and smiled. She couldn't wait to get away from San Antonio with her man. She hadn't lied. It had been too long since they'd taken their time in bed together. They'd made love, but it'd been rushed, both of them feeling vulnerable with the threat hanging over their heads. She couldn't wait to be with Daxton with no worries between them, other than pleasuring each other.

* * *

DAX ENTERED Mack's office building with large strides. He hadn't heard from her in a couple of hours, which wasn't too concerning since she'd told him at lunch she had a lot of work to do before they could leave. He didn't want to rush to conclusions, but after a week and a half of nothing remotely concerning happening, he'd told himself that Mack was fine at work. He'd tried calling once, but her phone went to voice mail. Dax rationalized it by telling himself she was working extra hard to be able to get away for the long weekend. But now, as he strode into her building, he felt very uncomfortable about his decision to not check on her earlier.

The other employees knew who he was by now and greeted him easily as he walked through the office. Dax didn't see Mack's boss anywhere around. He stopped at Mack's office and looked inside. Empty. He turned around and headed for the administrative assistant who sat a couple of cubicles away.

"Hey, Sandra, have you seen Mack?"

"Actually, no. She told me she was going to take a quick break and she didn't come back. I figured she'd called you and decided to leave early. We all heard about the awesome weekend you have planned. Mackenzie told us all about it."

Dax frowned. "When did she take the break?"

Sandra looked down at her watch. "Probably about two hours ago, I guess."

Fuck. Two hours. Dax turned and strode quickly back to Mackenzie's office. He rounded her desk and opened the drawer where he'd seen her stash her purse. It was there. He looked around her desk. Mack's cell phone was sitting next to her keyboard. He wiggled the mouse, the monitor came to life, and Dax could see that Mackenzie had locked her computer, following proper office protocol. It looked as though she'd simply left her office for a quick break as she told Sandra she was going to do.

Dax's stomach churned. He tried to hold himself together. No, this wasn't anything. Mackenzie knew to be careful. She was fine. Dax pocketed her cell phone and went back to Sandra's desk.

"Where would she go to take a break?"

Sandra got up immediately. "Let me show you, it'll be quicker."

Dax nodded and followed behind Sandra as she led the way down a hall into a small break room. It was at the end of the building. Dax looked around. There were three small tables in the area, each with four chairs. Against the wall were two soda machines and a snack machine. Against the wall perpendicular to the vending machines was a sink, cabinets, a water cooler filled with water, and a plastic bin filled with plastic forks and spoons and a handful of napkins. A trash can sat, half-filled, next to the sink. Nothing looked out of place.

Dax stepped out of the room and looked around. To the right was a hallway leading to another room full of cubicles. To the left were two doors. He stepped to the first and opened it cautiously. It was a janitor's closet. Inside was a bucket and a mop as well as a cleaning cart. The room was tidy and neat. Dax closed the door and walked to the other door.

It opened to a stairwell.

The uneasy feeling inside Dax bloomed until it filled his throat. While there was security in the lobby on the first floor of the building, Dax hadn't been able to get 24/7 security for Mack. He'd been cocky, thinking he'd covered the main entrance and exit and she'd be fine. He'd been stupid. Dax turned to Sandra. "I need you to find me *anyone* who saw Mackenzie this afternoon. I need to know the last time anyone saw her and what they saw her doing."

"Yes, sir." Sandra could obviously feel the waves of danger emanating from Daxton as he went into full Ranger mode. She turned around immediately to do as he'd asked.

Dax took out his phone and swiped it on and hit Cruz's name. As soon as Cruz picked up, Dax started talking.

"He's got Mack. I don't know how yet, but dammit, Cruz. I need you."

"Where are you?" Cruz didn't waste time asking how he knew Mackenzie had been taken. He got right to business.

"I'm at her office. No one has seen her in a couple of hours. The secretary said Mack told her she was going to take a break. The break room is next to a set of stairs."

"I'm on my way. Don't let anyone touch anything.

If the Reaper did get to her, that place is now a crime scene."

"Fuck."

"Stay with me, Dax."

"That fucker has her."

"Dax." Cruz said his name as a warning.

Dax took a deep breath, knowing he had to keep his emotions in check. "I'm fine. Just get here."

"On my way."

The line went dead. Dax knew Cruz would call Quint and there'd be people crawling all over the office before too long. Knowing if he stopped to think too much, he'd lose it, Dax headed back to Sandra.

She'd done what he'd asked her to do and there was a large crowd of people standing around her desk.

One of the women spoke in a nasally voice. "Look, I'm sorry Mack skipped out on you, but my employees have work to do. They can't just drop everything just because you told them to."

Knowing this was Mack's boss he'd heard so much about, Dax said curtly, "Nancy, right?" At her nod, he continued in a pissed-off voice. "Mackenzie is missing. I'm very sorry if your first concern isn't for her, but for work. Shit, woman, you work in a nonprofit organization that's supposed to help people. Shut the hell up and help me help Mack. If you haven't seen her, fine, get the fuck out and let me talk to everyone else. I'm sure after I talk to them, they can go back to doing the precious work that you take credit for. Now, can I continue, or do you want to keep antagonizing me when Mack could be suffering at the hands of a psycho serial killer?"

The room was silent. No one said a word as they watched Nancy try to think of something to say to backtrack. Finally she said quietly, "Please continue," and then she turned around, her hair swishing around her, and went back to her office, shutting the door behind her. Not stopping to think about how much Mack would've loved seeing her boss eat a slice of humble pie, Dax turned to the employees.

"Listen, everyone. Please. First, don't touch anything unnecessarily. Keep away from the break room. The FBI and the SAPD are on their way. I'm sure the officers will interview you, but please, think hard. When was the last time you saw Mackenzie today? Did anyone see anything that seemed out of place?"

Dax watched as each of the employees shrugged and shook their head. From what he could gather, the last time anyone saw Mack was around a quarter past three that afternoon. It was now half past four.

Two fucking hours. That bastard had had her for two hours. It was time enough for him to have her long gone from the area.

The phone in Dax's front pocket buzzed. It was Mackenzie's cell, not his own.

Dax pulled it out with clenched teeth, dread filling his gut. He swiped it, not needing the password to see the text that had just been sent. The three words seared themselves onto his brain and Dax couldn't hold back a small whimper.

Game on Ranger

CHAPTER 13

Two o'clock AM

DAX PACED the small office in the Ranger Station, barely holding himself together. It was probably about eleven hours after the Reaper had kidnapped Mackenzie. Quint, Cruz, and TJ, as well as Hayden, who worked for the Bexar County Sheriff's Office, were all there with him. Conor, a Game Warden and a member of the SCOUT team, had also heard about Mack's disappearance and had shown up. Also present were about five other random employees of the FBI office and the SAPD. Papers were strewn over the large conference table, the voices were low and rumbled as the men and women frantically tried to find something, anything, that they might have missed that would lead them to the killer, and the man who'd kidnapped one of their own.

Dax stopped in front of the large picture window overlooking the parking lot, putting his hands on the sill and leaned over, staring out into the night, but not seeing anything. The only thing he could picture was Mack's smile. Scenes flitted through his mind as if he was watching a movie.

Mack in bed smiling up at him. Mack in his car, holding his hand while gesturing wildly with the other as she rambled on about something. Mack in his shower. Mack at his kitchen table. Mack. Fuck.

Dax jerked when TJ put his hand on his shoulder. He turned eagerly to his friend. "Got anything?"

TJ just shook his head. "Nothing more than we had a few hours ago."

Dax turned back to the window. "I never thought I'd find the woman who was meant for me, TJ. I'd resigned myself to being alone. Mack came barreling into my life with her oddball charm and her quirky sense of humor and I haven't been the same since. I've lost her."

"No! Don't fucking say that, Dax. You haven't lost her. Don't give up now. For Christ's sake, man, Mackenzie *needs* you. You can't give up on her."

Dax turned in frustration and threw his hand out, indicating the table and all the people. "We've been at it for hours, and we have nothing. *Nothing.* How in the hell are we supposed to catch this guy when we don't know jack shit about him? He's been two steps ahead of us the entire time. It's been around eleven hours, TJ. Eleven. Fucking. Hours. She could be buried five feet underground by now. We'll never find her unless he wants to fuck with me."

TJ, for once, didn't have any words of comfort for his friend. "Come on back to the table; let's look over the cemeteries where the other women were found again, we have to be missing some sort of pattern."

TJ watched as Dax nodded and turned away again, but not before TJ saw a tear fall over Dax's cheek. He squeezed his friend's shoulder and went back to the table, leaving Dax to get control over his grief.

SEVEN THIRTY AM

DAX STARED bleary-eyed at the transcripts of tips sitting in front of him that had been called into the various law enforcement offices. The sun was peeking over the horizon, making for a beautiful sunrise. Dax could feel the heat on his face through the window, but didn't bother looking up. He only cared about Mackenzie right now. Not eating, not sleeping, not a fucking sunrise.

Quint and Cruz were snoring in the seats next to him. Quint had succumbed to sleep around four thirty and Cruz not much later. They were the only ones left in the big conference room at Ranger Company F. Dax knew his fellow Rangers would soon be arriving, and they'd put all their other cases on hold for him...for Mack...but his skin was crawling. He was on the verge of something, but he couldn't quite grab ahold of it. It was there. He'd read something in the hundreds of pages of transcribed phone calls and tips they'd received after the FBI profilers had gone to the media and reported on the profile of the Lone Star Reaper.

Dax flipped through the page and scanned the information he was seeing through blurry eyes. He needed coffee, but it'd have to wait. The feeling hadn't started until recently, so he went back and looked at the latest couple of tips.

MY NEIGHBOR HAS to be the Lone Star Reaper, because he's extra creepy. I wish he'd move.

· · ·

197

I'VE SEEN this guy at the grocery store and he seems to fit the profile the guy on television talked about. He's middle age and he always buys olives. I mean cans and cans of olives. That's crazy! I bet he's the killer.

I WORKED with a guy who just seemed off. We were the night custodians for this big building and even though we used cleansers all the time, his hands were always dirty. He didn't socialize with any of the rest of us at all. It was weird.

I'M afraid the Reaper could be my husband. He works late every weekend but gets texts at weird times and won't let me see them. He smells like perfume too. I bet it's those missing women's perfume.

DAX SLAMMED the notebook shut and threw it across the table, watching as it came to rest on the other side, just shy of tumbling over the edge. He shut his eyes and leaned back in his chair. The leather creaked under him as the chair rocked back with his body weight. He put the heels of his hands into his eyes and rubbed.

People just didn't get it. Mackenzie's life was held

in the palms of their hands, and they were reporting cheating husbands and creepy co-workers as the Reaper. It was maddening. Wait a minute…

Dax suddenly shot forward in his chair, his hands hitting the top of the table with a loud smack, waking up both Cruz and Quint. Dax quickly leaned up out of his chair and across the table, snatching up the notebook he'd just thrown.

"Oh my fucking God. That has to be a clue."

"What? Dax? What time is it?"

Dax ignored Quint's drowsy murmurings and frantically flipped back through the tips, trying to find the one he wanted.

He stopped at the one he was looking for and flipped it over to Cruz. "Read that."

Cruz didn't hesitate, and seemed to come awake immediately. He leaned over and read the tip Dax was referring to. He looked up. "Maybe."

Dax stood and started pacing again. "I know you think I'm desperate and am seeing clues where there might not be any. But this seems promising. He worked nights. He was a janitor. He had time to get to those women during the day when he wasn't working. We need to go back through and see if we can't match up the victims with this guy. And Mack. No one notices the cleaning crew in buildings. What if he was there yesterday? Mack is nice to everyone.

She would've taken the time to talk to this guy, to try to befriend him. He could've done something and sneaked her out of the building by the stairs next to the break room. Hell, he probably has a van or something that wouldn't seem out of place either."

Cruz pulled the tip sheet closer to him, thinking out loud. "His dirty hands could be because of the dirt and burying the boxes, and it matches the profile." He stood up and took the notebook with him. "I'll get the tipster on the line right away. We need to get more information. We need to know what this guy's name is."

"Once you get the name, I'll see if I can't get the forensic team to research where he might have worked as well. It could lead to a pattern of where he got his victims from," Quint added, standing up himself, all signs of being sleepy gone from his face. "It could take awhile, but I'll see what I can do to get them to put a rush on it."

Dax took a deep breath before following his friends out of the room. It might be nothing, but it was more than they'd had an hour ago. He put his hand in his pocket and pulled out Mack's cell phone. He absently tapped the screen and glared down at the words, still showing on the opening screen. He knew Mack's password, but couldn't bring himself to use it.

Game on Ranger

The words sat on the screen, mocking Dax.

What was the bastard waiting for? Why hadn't he contacted him? Dax figured the Reaper knew where he was and probably had all of his own personal contact information as well. If he wanted to play a fucking game with Mack's life, why hadn't he started it already?

Dax shoved the phone back into his pocket and strode out of the room behind his friends. He had some research to do. He'd catch this motherfucker if it was the last thing he ever did. If he killed Mackenzie, and at this point it was a likely ending to the whole fucked-up mess, Dax knew he'd make the Reaper pay. The Reaper would wish he hadn't laid his eyes on Dax or Mackenzie.

It wouldn't bring her back, but it'd make Dax feel better…maybe.

Ten o'clock AM

QUINT BURST into Dax's office holding a piece of paper. "Jordan Charles Staal. Age thirty-nine. Has a high school education. Was married for two years to a second cousin. She disappeared and her information is sitting in the cold-case files. What do you want to bet he killed her? We're still working on finding out about his childhood, looking for signs of abuse or any kind of juvenile record."

Dax sat up straight in his chair and drilled Quint with his eyes. "Jobs?" he barked.

Quint sat on the edge of the wooden chair in front of Dax's desk and continued. "He's held six different custodian jobs in the last eight years. All like the tipster said, third shift. We're cross-referencing the victims now, but I recognize at least one of the buildings off the top of my head as where the fourth victim worked." Quint looked up. "We've fucking got him, Dax."

"It seems too easy."

"Don't think that. We'll get him, and Mackenzie too."

TWO O'CLOCK PM

THE RANGER SPECIAL RESPONSE TEAM spread out around the ramshackle house in western San Antonio. The neighborhood looked as though it once used to be pretty, but now the houses mostly appeared abandoned and almost all needed some sort of major repair.

Dax didn't see any of that. He was fixated on the door in front of him. They'd tracked Staal's address through his employment records and as soon as they'd gathered the SRT, they were on their way.

Dax had agreed not to be at the forefront of the assault; he was too close to the case. He watched as the door was broken in and the team rushed into the house. He followed behind, gun drawn, hoping against hope they'd find Staal cowering in a back room and he'd tell them what he did with Mack.

It was quickly clear that no one had lived in the house in a very long time. It smelled stale and there were cobwebs everywhere. Some kids had obviously broken in and partied in the house at one point, as there were beer cans strewn all over the floor.

The address Staal had given his employers was false. No one was there. Not Staal, and not Mackenzie.

Dax's stomach churned. Mack wasn't here and he had no idea where she was. He wasn't sure he'd ever see Mack alive again. He'd promised he'd keep her safe and he'd let her down.

Four Thirty PM

. . .

DAX WATCHED the news correspondent review the facts of the Reaper case dispassionately.

AND NOW AN UPDATE to the killer the press has dubbed the Lone Star Reaper. It's being reported that another woman is missing. Mackenzie Morgan, age thirty-seven, disappeared from her workplace yesterday afternoon. The San Antonio Police Department, the Texas Rangers and the FBI are working on a joint operation to follow any leads.

We've been told they have a person of interest in the case. Jordan Charles Staal. If you have any information about Mr. Staal's whereabouts, or if you have information that might lead to finding him so he can be questioned, please call the police department's tip line at...

DAX CLICKED OFF THE TELEVISION, not able to stomach the sight of Staal's face. The third place the man had worked was able to provide them with his picture from the employee ID computer system. He truly was a creepy-looking man. He had black hair that was too long. His jaw was tight and he wasn't smiling in the photo. There was a scar running along the right side of his face, from the corner of his mouth all the way up to disappear into his hairline.

Dax closed his eyes. He was so tired, but didn't know if he could sleep. He knew he couldn't go back to his apartment. He'd see Mack's stuff, see the indentation in the pillow where she'd last lain her head, he'd smell her perfume and soap in the bathroom, smell her vanilla scent all over his apartment. Nope, he'd have to see if he could catch a few hours of sleep here at his desk instead.

Even though it wasn't even five in the afternoon yet, Dax crossed his arms and put them on his desktop. He put his head down and closed his eyes, willing the tears back. If he let them out now, he didn't know if he'd be able to stop.

Six Thirty PM

DAX JERKED up from his awkward position and looked around in confusion. He hadn't slept well; visions of Mackenzie crying out for him in a dark room haunted him. He couldn't find her and she needed him. He rubbed his hand over his eyes, trying to orient himself.

The cell phone in his back pocket vibrated again. Dax pulled it out and saw the number was blocked. Normally he'd let the call go to voice mail, but while

Mackenzie was missing, he wasn't taking any chances.

"Chambers."

"Daxton?"

Dax straightened his spine then stood up suddenly and headed out of his office. He had to get someone...anyone. Holy fucking shit. Mack was on the phone.

"Mack? Where are you, sweetheart? I'm on my way to you right now, just tell me where you are and I'll come get you."

Her voice was low and strained and the connection was crap. The air crackled and dropped in and out as she spoke the words Dax somehow knew, from the very fiber of his being, were coming.

"I don't know. I'm buried alive."

CHAPTER 14

DAX HAD BEEN on the move before Mackenzie had spoken, but he halted for a moment, holding himself upright in the hallway of his office building with a hand on the wall. He lowered his head in despair. He then took a deep breath and strode down the hall with purpose. It might be evening, but the building was never empty. He wasn't hanging up with Mackenzie to try to get ahold of someone; he'd just have to multitask.

"Mack..." Dax stopped. He didn't really know what to say. What the hell *did* you say to someone who was in her situation? He tried to think. He had to pull his head out of his ass and *think*.

"I love you." First things first. He had to tell Mack how much he cared about her.

"I love you too, Daxton. I...know how it happened...drink...woke up."

"You're cutting in and out, baby. Try again."

Dax burst into the Major's office and put his hand over the speaker on his phone. "Mack's on the phone. She's underground somewhere. Get Cruz and Quint on the line, now."

The Major didn't hesitate. He immediately picked up the phone on his desk and dialed.

Mackenzie's voice was small and wobbly in Dax's ear. He'd never heard her sound so unsure. "I know how he got me. I was...work, the janitor...a glass of water, and I woke up...the dark. It's so dark, Daxton."

Dax backed away from the Major's desk and turned toward the window. Not seeing anything but Mackenzie's face, he tried to reassure her. "It's not your fault. It's mine. I shouldn't have let you keep working. I should've been there."

"No, Daxton. Don't do that. You couldn't know, there's no way...known this would happen."

"You're wrong, Mack. He knew about you, I should've protected you better."

"I know you told me never to get in a car with someone who wanted to...but does it count if I didn't...what was happening?"

The connection was crap, but Dax could get the

gist of what Mack was saying. "I think you get a pass, baby. He probably roofied your water."

"Yeah, I figured that too...seemed so nice. I hadn't seen him around...but he was getting his own cup of...he offered me one too, I said sure. I'm sorry, Daxton, I'm so fucking sorry."

"It's okay. It's okay. I'm going to find you. We know his name. Do you hear me? We know who he is."

"Good. You'll find me?"

Dax heard Mack's voice crack. He gripped his phone so hard he thought he'd break it. He breathed in through his nose trying to get his composure back. "I'll find you, baby. No matter what. I'll find you and bring you home."

Dax looked over at the Major. He was gesturing to his office door. Dax followed him out and back toward the conference room.

"Look at the phone in your hand, Mack. Take it away from your ear for a second and tell me if you can see a phone number on it. The number was blocked from my end, so I can't call you back if we lose the connection."

"Don't go, Daxton! Oh God, please...don't—"

"Mackenzie!" Dax's tone was harsh. He was losing her and he needed her focused on helping him find her. "Listen to me. You there? You listening?"

"I'm here."

"Take a deep breath, sweetheart. Don't panic. If you panic, you'll lose too much air. Do you understand? You have to stay as calm as you can. If we lose the connection, don't freak. You called me, right? All you have to do is call me back. I'll be here."

"Yeah, okay, you're right. I'm...hang on and let me...if I can see the number."

There was a pause and Dax figured Mack was looking at the face of the phone; he turned to the Major. "What's their ETA?"

"They're on their way, lights and sirens, and I put the SRT on standby. As soon as we get *any* information, we're ready to roll."

Mackenzie's voice came back over the line. "I don't see the number. I clicked buttons but...light. It's so dark. I can't find...I can't find it."

"Okay. Don't worry about it. If we lose the connection, you can just call me back. I'm not going to hang up. You might hear me talking to others in the background, but I'm still here. Okay?"

"Okay."

"I'm going to get to you, Mack. I need you to tell me everything you can about what you remember, what you see, smell, hear, and what you feel around you. Everything, Mack. No matter how small you think it is. How insignificant. Every single thing will help me get to you."

Mackenzie's description of her surroundings was completely heartbreaking and Dax couldn't hold back the tears that had been at the back of his throat since he'd answered the phone and heard Mack's voice. She was trying to be so brave and he couldn't fucking stand it.

"I'm pretty sure…in a coffin. There's no material, it's all wood, but…only a couple inches above…head but it seems like…room at my feet. For the first time…glad to be short."

Dax grabbed a tissue from the box in the middle of the conference table and turned his back to the Major. He held the tissue to his eyes, willing himself to keep silent. Mackenzie didn't need to hear him losing it.

"It's crude…I think. There's no material…I admit I freaked out when…and in places…nails. I found this phone and…when…it…later."

Dax cleared his throat. "Mack, say again. That last part cut out." He was proud at how normal his voice sounded.

"The phone was here and two bottles of water. I thought I'd save them for later."

"Good thinking, Mack. What do you hear?"

Mackenzie's voice lowered. "Nothing. There's

nothing. It's so quiet all I can hear is the ringing in my ears."

"What about smell? What do you smell?" Dax knew even the most insignificant thing could be the difference between finding Staal and thus, Mack...or not finding either of them.

"Dirt. Daxton, I smell dirt. I'm so scared...I thought I'd be brave, but I can't..."

Dax's heart felt as if it was being pulled out of his body, it hurt so badly. Hearing Mackenzie break down into sobs was completely heart wrenching.

"Shhhh, baby. Deep breaths. I know you're scared. I am too. I'm doing everything I can to find you. You hear me? Don't give up on me."

As Mackenzie tried to control her sobs, Dax heard the door open. Quint and Cruz stalked in, crazed looks in their eyes.

"That her?" Quint asked.

Dax nodded.

"That your cell? The guys are seeing if they can trace it," Cruz told Dax matter-of-factly.

Dax nodded again, relieved as fuck his friends were there.

"She give you anything yet?"

Dax held up his finger to tell Quint to wait a second. He spoke into the phone again. "Mack?

Quint and Cruz are here; can you give me a moment to talk to them?"

"Yeah. I'm okay. Talk...them." Mackenzie's voice was a bit stronger this time.

"I'm so fucking proud of you, sweetheart. I can still hear you, but I'm going to put you on mute a second. I'm not hanging up. Okay? Hang on."

Dax kept the phone against his ear, not willing to be out of hearing distance from Mackenzie for even a second, just in case she needed him.

"She's in a homemade wooden box, sounds like the others, two water bottles, cell phone. She can't hear anything, but can smell dirt. Bastard must've drugged her. She saw him in the break room and he got her a glass of water. It's about the last thing she remembers. I don't think she's going to be able to give us anything." Dax paused, meeting his friends' eyes. "Help me. For God's sake, help me."

"Tips are rolling in from tonight's news. We're following up on them now."

"It needs to be faster, Quint."

Quint simply nodded, went to the table, pulled out his phone and punched some buttons.

Dax didn't see what Cruz was doing, but turned his attention back to Mack and clicked the mute button so she could hear him again. "I'm back, sweetheart."

"Daxton?"

"Yeah, Mack. I'm here."

"Does my family know…?"

"Yeah, they know." Dax had fielded a call from her brother Mark before he'd taken the short catnap. He'd been furious, rightly so, and Dax had promised him they were doing everything they could to find his sister. Dax knew his words weren't comforting in the least to the man, because they weren't to his own ears.

"Don't let them see…scene photos. I don't want them…me looking…this."

"Fuck, baby."

"Promise," she demanded.

"I promise."

"Do you remember…first kiss?"

"How could I forget?"

"You pushed me up against the wall and were trying…scare me. I told you I wasn't…and you leaned down…kissed me. I didn't tell…that if you'd asked, I would've…dragged…hall to my…and made love to you right then. You smell fantastic…I ever tell you that before? Well…do. I love the way…smell. Like man and…you should bottle that shit, you'd…a mint on it. But I want to keep it…myself. I'd give anything…smell you…now."

Dax shut his eyes, loving how Mack could ramble

even when she was scared out of her mind and buried underground. "I remember that night. I couldn't have stopped myself from kissing you if my job depended on it. You were so cute, and not scared of me in the least. And Mack, you might think I smell good, but you...you corner the market on that. Every morning before I get out of bed I lean into you and bury my nose in your hair. It's vanilla or something. I don't know exactly what it is, but it's you. And I love it."

"Really?"

"Really."

Dax noticed Cruz gesturing to him frantically from the table.

"Hang on, Mack. Okay? I gotta talk to Cruz."

"Okay. It's not like...going anywhere."

Dax chuckled, even though there wasn't anything to laugh about, and took the four steps over to Cruz. He held his hand over the speaker on the phone.

"What you got?"

"One of the tips came from a funeral director. He'd been watching the news and recognized Staal. Said he's seen him a few times at various visitation services to 'pay his respects.' I'm figuring Staal doesn't even know the people in the visitations, he just goes to get off on seeing the dead bodies in the coffins laid out."

Dax saw where Cruz was going. "So we just narrowed down the area where he might live."

"Right."

Quint was speaking into his phone, ordering whoever was on the other end to "hurry it up."

"Daxton?"

Dax turned his attention away from his friends and back to Mackenzie immediately. "Yeah, sweetheart?"

Her words were coming in pants now. Dax tried not to panic. He was running out of time, dammit.

"I don't regret meeting you."

"Baby—"

"No, really. Even if I knew how this would end up when we first met, I'd still...through with it. I've been happier in the last...months than I have in my...life. I know I'm not perfect, hell...a pain in the ass. I hadn't met one...who could put...me. But you, you just ignored...I got bitchy and you smirked at me. It was annoying...first, but you made me really think. I don't...care if you put the...in pointy side up. It's stupid...argue over something...that. I want you to know that I don't regret a...thing about...you. I know what love is now, and...cherish that."

"Mack."

"No, I'm still talking."

Dax smiled sadly again and lowered his head. Fuck. She was killing him.

"Don't let this prevent...trying again. You found love once, you'll...again. And don't tell me...too old. That's bullshit. You should...a chance. Don't stop living just because I did."

"Fuck!" The word was torn from Dax's mouth and he couldn't take it anymore. He took a step to the table, handed his cell to Cruz, and left the conference room.

CHAPTER 15

MACKENZIE TRIED to hold back her sobs, but couldn't. She'd meant every word she'd said to Daxton. She didn't regret one second of their relationship, even though it led to her being buried alive. It wasn't Daxton's fault and she wouldn't have given up the feeling of being loved, and loving in return, for anything.

She hadn't meant to upset Daxton, but she knew she had to say the words. She hoped he'd forgive her.

Mackenzie was uncomfortable. She'd been lying in the same position for way too long. She couldn't sit up, she couldn't turn over, the space she was in was simply too small. She'd tried to turn on her side, but couldn't. Her hips hurt, her butt hurt, and she was scared out of her mind. She also knew she was dying.

The air in the coffin was getting thin. Mackenzie could tell because she found herself panting more and more as she spoke with Daxton. She had no idea how long she'd been in there. She'd been completely freaked when she'd come to the first time and found herself unable to move. She'd panicked and whacked her head against the top of the box more than once while she was freaking out. She must've passed out, but once she'd woken up and calmed down, Mack had known immediately what had happened.

The fucking janitor.

He hadn't even given her a chance to fight him. The drugs made her groggy and uncoordinated and he was practically carrying her by the time they'd gotten to the bottom of the stairs. Mackenzie didn't remember anything after that, and she'd come to in the box. It could've been an hour, or three days. Mack simply had no idea.

She'd flailed around in the coffin for way too long before taking a deep breath to calm herself down. She'd fumbled around, trying to feel around her, and had discovered the bottles of water and the phone sitting next to her shoulders. The bastard had known she wouldn't be able to reach them if they were at her feet.

Mackenzie tried to talk to Daxton. "Hello? Daxton? Are you there?"

"Hey, Mackenzie, it's Cruz."

"Where's Daxton?"

"He's taking a break, he'll be right back. How're you holding up?"

"Cruz, I'm not going to make...I'm having a hard time breathing...just know I'm not...survive."

"Don't think that way. We're close to figuring this out. Don't give up on us."

"I'm...practical. Please, promise...don't let Daxton become...hermit. Make him...out and meet...don't let him...alone for the...life. I couldn't stand...please?"

"I won't, Mackenzie. I promise."

"Thank you. I...a question."

"Anything."

"How the hell am I able...to you on a fucking cell...if I'm underground?"

Cruz froze. Holy hell. How the fuck had he overlooked that?

Mackenzie continued. Cruz could understand her through the crappy connection...barely.

"I mean, doesn't dirt...connection? It doesn't make...that I'd be...get a connection...I was underground. Right? Hell, I once...call Mark while I was...car going through...tunnel and...call totally dropped...in the middle...conversation. Of course... blamed me and told me...trying to avoid...to him but I told him…was crap that it was…I was underground. I thought…it now and I don't…it."

"Listen to me, Mackenzie. Are you listening?" At her affirmative response, Cruz continued. "We're on the verge of finding out where this guy lives. We're going to get to his house as soon as we figure it out. We'll get him and he'll tell us where you are. Maybe you're not underground yet; maybe he's stashed that coffin somewhere until he can get back to the cemetery to bury it. That's why you can talk on the cell. I don't know. But even if you're underground, you hold on. Got it? Breathe slowly, do whatever you have to do, but hold the fuck on. You aren't allowed to give up. Not when we're this close. Hear me?"

"You're not…saying that? You really are…the way?"

"We really are." Cruz forgave himself the slight lie. They weren't on their way to anywhere at the moment. They still needed more information.

"I wish there was more I could do to help you guys. I feel worthless…here. If I was a true heroine… all sorts of information to give…that would lead you right to me."

"Don't worry about it, Mackenzie. It's our job to do that. Your only job is to wait for us to get there. And to keep breathing. Nothing else."

"Okay. Is Daxton there?"

"Not yet, but he will be soon."

"Okay."

Quint hung up the phone he'd been on and swore. Cruz turned his head toward him with raised eyebrows. "Where's Dax? He needs to get his ass in here. There's a development."

Just as the words left Quint's mouth, Dax walked back in. The knuckles on his left hand were bloody, but no one said a word about it. It was obvious Dax had heard Quint's words, but he still went straight to Cruz and held out his hand for the phone. Cruz handed it to him immediately.

"Mack?"

"Yeah…here."

"Okay, hang on, I gotta talk to Quint. He's got an update for us. We're getting closer. I swear."

"I know. I'll be here when you find me, Daxton."

Dax muted the phone again and turned to Quint.

"A call just came in on the tip line. I'm going to read you what the caller said." Quint looked Dax in the eyes. "Keep it locked down, Dax. Mackenzie needs you."

Dax clenched his teeth. He had no idea how much more he could take. He nodded.

"The caller's voice wasn't altered this time. It was a man. He said, and I quote, 'Jordan Staal here. I hope Ranger Chambers is having a good time talking with his lover. It really was too easy to get to her. He should watch over those he loves better. And the memory of that first kiss is gonna have to be enough to tide him over for the rest of his life. Too bad he didn't fuck her that first night.'"

The room was silent after Quint's voice faded, until Dax broke it. "That fucker is listening. He put the damn phone in there with her so he could listen to her calling me."

No one said anything. The level of Staal's cruelty was becoming clearer as the minutes went by.

The ringing of Cruz's cell phone broke the heavy atmosphere of the room. "Livingston. Yeah. Got it. Meet at Ranger Company in ten. Out."

Cruz kept his voice low. "The SRT is ready. We have an address. Fucker screwed up. Gave a different address to the first company he worked at. It's the same address his wife was reported missing from. It's him this time. I can feel it. We're headed out in ten. We're going to get your woman, Dax."

Dax nodded once and was on the move before Cruz had finished speaking. Ten minutes, it felt like ten hours. He clicked the phone off mute once again. "Mack?"

"...you find me yet?" Her voice was soft, but steely. It was obvious Mackenzie was scared out of her mind, but she was keeping a lock on it. She was hanging in there, believing he was coming for her.

"We're working on it." Dax didn't want to say anything to alert Staal they were on their way right then to get him. He hated knowing that asshole was listening to his conversation with Mack, but he couldn't let her know. Dax knew he had to act like he had no idea. Keeping it from Mack made him feel like shit, but he didn't have a choice. Dax wanted to give her some hope, something to give her so she'd hang on until he could get to her. He took a breath and lobbed a Hail Mary, hoping she'd figure out what he was saying. "Remember when we had that conversation about Christmas, sweetheart?"

"Uh, no."

"You know, you were telling me about the time Matthew brought you downstairs to the closet and told you that your parents were Santa Claus? You said you cried for a bit until he showed you how to unwrap just the end of the packages so you could see what was inside, then you could close it back up and no one would know you peeked?"

Mackenzie closed her eyes and tried to remember back to any conversation she'd had with Daxton about Christmas... Finally she remembered. They'd been talking about anticipation and how Mackenzie had no patience. She hated knowing she had to wait for something. She'd told Daxton she always preferred to be surprised than to know something was coming. Vacations, presents, holidays…they were all torture, knowing they were coming but not there yet.

"Oh, yeah, I remember now."

"Well, this is like that." Dax hoped like hell Mack understood what he so badly was trying to say.

Mackenzie frantically tried to read between the lines of what Daxton was saying. It was obvious he was trying to tell her something. "Okay, Daxton." She thought about it…she thought he was saying that she had to hold on…have patience because he was on his way. It wouldn't be a surprise; he was coming. She got that. Mackenzie decided right then and there anticipation wasn't necessarily a bad thing.

"Okay, Mack. Cruz has his technicians working as hard as they can. We've almost got it. Swear. You just hold on. Baby? I have to put the phone on mute on my end, but I can still hear you. Okay? Just keep talking to me. I can hear you just fine. Whatever you need to say, say it."

Mackenzie didn't want Daxton to put her on mute. She wanted to close her eyes and hear the low rumble of his voice as he spoke with her. The silence pressed in on her when he muted his end of the line, making her tomb seem even smaller than it was, but she answered affirmatively anyway. "Okay."

Mackenzie strained to hear anything on the other end of the line. She heard nothing. The coffin was airtight and completely silent. She started talking to break the silence; she couldn't just lie there in stillness.

Dax kept his phone at his ear, listening to Mack talk about nothing. Her voice still stuttered in and out, but Dax didn't care. She was talking, that meant she was breathing. He'd go with it. He opened the door to the garage, nodding in surprise at both Conor and TJ. They'd obviously been granted permission to be part of the entry team. He looked around in approval at the rest of the men assembled. The SRT was ready to go.

"I've sent the coordinates to Staal's house to your GPSs. We're going in silent. He's got ears on the phone call between Chambers and Ms. Morgan, so when Dax gives the cue, everyone shut the fuck up. We want to sneak up on him. He can't know we're on the way. Got it?" Cruz told the men waiting for the word to go in and arrest a killer.

There were nods all around. Dax put his cell on the trunk of the car in front of him while he shrugged on the bulletproof vest. He wouldn't be a part of the entry team, once again he'd leave that to

Cruz's people, but there was no way he wasn't going with them. He grabbed up the phone again and sat down in the front seat of Quint's patrol car.

Nine minutes. Dax would be able to look Jordan Charles Staal in the face in nine minutes and find out where he'd stashed his woman.

CHAPTER 16

"Did you cancel...reservations for the hotel in Austin? Cos you can't...waste the money. Make sure they...charge your card. Once I had a vacation planned...mom got sick...forgot to call and I had... dollar charge. They refused...take it off even... produced the doctor's bill...mom was sick. Bastards. So it might...seem like a lot, but you shouldn't let... get away with that shit. When you find me...we go there? It sounded...and I was looking forward...all weekend in bed...you."

Mackenzie paused and panted. She had no idea if Daxton was even listening to her anymore, but she didn't stop talking. Even though she was dizzy and her chest hurt to breathe, she didn't stop.

"I hate math. I don't know...I just do. I know we need...and...use it all the time but...suck at it. It's stupid...not that hard. But I just have never...how to do it in my head. I always...the wrong column and end up...the wrong answer. Thank...calculators. Where would we be without...? I use the app...all the time. It's embarrassing...break it out...day. I must look like...a six...kid."

Dax listened to Mack ramble on with clenched teeth. Her voice had gotten lower and lower and he hated it. He wanted to tell her to stop talking, to save her breath, and conserve the air in her tomb, but he couldn't make himself. Every word out of her mouth was being committed to his memory...just in case.

The vehicle stopped on a street in a nice neighborhood in northern San Antonio. The lawns were all well-kept and Dax could even see some people out playing in the yards. It wasn't the type of neighborhood he expected to see a scumbag like Staal living in. He tapped his phone to unmute it.

"Mack?"

"Daxton! I'm here, I'm here."

Dax's stomach hurt. Of course she was there. Where would she have gone? "I love you. You're doing great."

"I...it hurts to breathe."

Dax shut his eyes. Fuck. "I know, but keep doing it anyway. The forensics team just came in and I'm going to be busy for the next bit, but I'm not hanging up. But don't talk, baby. You need to save your air. Just relax for a bit, okay?"

"It's too quiet...ringing in my ears. I don't...it."

Knowing he wouldn't be able to reassure her for at least the next fifteen minutes or so, Dax suggested, "Would it help if I put my phone up to the radio? Then it wouldn't be quiet and you wouldn't waste your breath with talking."

"Yeah, I'd like that. As long as...not the god-awful silence."

"Okay, sweetheart. You know I love you, right? I'm gonna find you. Soon. You just have to hang on."

"I'll try, but...it's getting hard. If you don't...me, don't blame...I wouldn't change...about loving you. Not one thing. I've heard it doesn't hurt...you know...that I'll...basically fall asleep... The last thing...about is you. I'll remember the feel...hands on my body and...lips on mine. Don't mourn me forever, Daxton. That's an order."

Dax swallowed hard, ignoring the heavy hand Quint laid on his shoulder in silent support. "I'll love you forever, Mack. No one will come close to replacing you in my life and my heart. You're seriously the best thing that's ever happened to me. Ever. Hang in there for as long as you can...but if it gets too much and you need to fall asleep...it's okay.

Don't hang on for me if it hurts. You do what you need to do. I don't want you in pain. Got it?"

Dax could hear Mack sniff. Her words were just a wisp of sound. "I don't want to die. I want to live... fifty years with you."

"I know, Mack. I know. God, baby." Dax didn't know what to say. He sure as hell didn't want her to die either, but right this second, he had no idea how to prevent it. He was completely helpless to do anything for her, other than to try to reassure her.

"I love you, Daxton Chambers." Her words fortuitously didn't cut out.

Dax knew he had to get going. "I love you, too. I'm going to let you listen to some eighties music. Okay?" He heard her chuckle.

"Eighties music. What every girl stuck in...coffin wants to hear. It's fine. Anything...be okay, as long as it's not silence. Stay safe, Daxton. Don't...anything stupid."

Dax whispered his words. "I will. I love you, sweetheart." He didn't wait for her response, knowing it would tear his heart right out of his chest if he had to hear one more thing from her. He put his cell on the dash and took Quint's phone that he held out. He clicked on the music app, pulled up the eighties channel, and waited for the music to start. He placed Quint's phone face-down on his own, then closed his eyes, kissed his fingers and pressed them to the phones for a moment.

Abruptly he turned from the dashboard of the car and opened his door. He eased the door shut, making sure no sound could be heard over the phone lines, and nodded in approval as Quint did the same thing.

Neither man said a word as they got in position behind the Special Response Team. It was time to catch a rat in its hole...and hopefully pry the location of where he'd stashed Mackenzie out of him before it was too late.

DAX FOLLOWED the ten men into the small, nondescript house. They'd used the breaching tool to break down the front door and had swarmed inside, quickly fanning out to find where Staal was hiding. Within seconds, there were shouts from the back of the house. Dax moved that way with Quint and Cruz at his heels and stood in the doorway of what was obviously an office.

Staal was sitting behind three monitors with his hands on his head, grinning. He didn't bother to look at the officers who were pointing their AR15 rifles at him and ordering him to stand up and turn around. Cruz motioned for the officers to wait. Typically they would've grabbed him and cuffed him, but at the moment Staal had the upper hand. They didn't know if he was armed, and they needed information from him. They'd give him space until they had to make a move. At the moment he didn't look like a threat to them. They had to get him to talk.

"Well, well, well. Look who finally tracked me down. Took you long enough, Ranger Chambers."

"Shut the fuck up, Staal. Where is she?"

"Who? Oh…poor little Mackenzie?"

"You know that's who I'm talking about. Stand up and turn around, asshole."

"Tsk, tsk, tsk. You didn't think the game would be over that soon, did you? You really thought I'd stand up quaking in my boots and tell you where she was? That would ruin the fun now, wouldn't it?"

"Why are you doing this?" Cruz demanded, impatience in his voice.

"Why not?"

"That's not a fucking answer, Staal."

Staal's voice lost some of its easiness. "You want to know why? Haven't your precious profilers figured it out yet? Where'd you get them anyway? Profilers-R-Us? They don't know shit."

"Why don't you tell us then?" Dax tried to keep

calm, when all he wanted to do was reach across the desk, over the fucking monitors blocking his view, and choke the shit out of the man.

"You ever seen anyone die, Chambers? I mean, not because you shot them from ten feet away, but watched them moment by moment as they took their last breath? It's absolutely fascinating. If you watch closely enough, you can see the life literally drain from their eyes. I didn't understand it at first. My mother did though. She made me see."

"What are you talking about? Come on, stand up, and turn the fuck around." Quint's voice was testy.

"Oh, Officer Axton, you have no patience. My mother always told me I was the most patient little boy she'd ever seen. She taught me everything she knew. First, it was my little brother. He wouldn't shut up, you see. So she had to shut him up. She made me stand in the corner of the room and watch. She put her hand over his mouth and nose. He wiggled a bit and made some grunts, but eventually he quieted. It was beautiful. His little eyes were glazed and staring at the ceiling. I was afraid at first, but mother made me touch him, made me see how beautiful it was."

"Motherfucker." The officer standing next to Dax breathed the words almost tonelessly.

"And it was beautiful, but she showed me that

doing it that way was too easy. She trained me. She showed me how it worked. She'd hold me down in the tub, making me look her in the eyes as she held me underwater. Just when I didn't think I could hold my breath anymore, she'd let me up. She went to an estate sale one year and bought a brand-new coffin. It was a piece of beauty. I wish I still had it today... but I'm getting ahead of myself.

"Mother would put me in it and close it up, leaving me there for what seemed like hours on end, but was probably only twenty minutes at a time. She showed me what it meant, how it worked. How beautiful death could be. The more I struggled, the better it was. She got me a birthday present when I was just six years old. We lived in a crappy neighborhood with crackhead parents who didn't watch their kids. There was a little girl, Dorothy Allen. I'll never forget her. She trusted me. I told her we were playing a game. She climbed into that coffin all on her own. Mother and I listened as she cried and beat on the lid for two hours. Mother walked me through what was happening. She understood. Finally when the fervor died down and no one cared about finding Dorothy anymore, mother let me open the lid. I've never experienced anything like I did with her that first time."

Dax was appalled. Staal was sicker than they'd

imagined. "Where. Is. Mackenzie?" Dax bit the words out, not wanting to hear the filth spewing from Staal's mouth anymore.

"Calm down, she's right here, Ranger Chambers." Staal reached out and turned one of the three computer monitors around until Dax could see what Staal had been watching. It was grainy, and had a greenish hue to it, but everyone in the room could see what it was. It was Mackenzie. Inside a box.

"She's beautiful. So much more than any of the others. And I've come so far since Mother taught me what she knew. When she couldn't teach me anything else, I put *her* in our coffin and listened as *she* died a beautiful death. I've honed my craft. The water gives them hope, makes them hold on just a little bit longer. Prolonging their deaths. I tried using a walkie-talkie, but that didn't work at all, not enough range. I then found that using a special satellite phone, with extra strength, used by the toughest military teams in the world, was the key."

Staal leaned over and pushed a button on a small console on his desk. The haunting notes of Bonnie Tyler's "Total Eclipse of the Heart" sounded loud in the room. "Your last words to each other were beautiful. Epic. That's what I'd been missing with all the others. They died, but no one knew. With Mackenzie, you knew. She knows she's dying. You know she's dying. You gave her permission to die. Fucking perfect. You told her to die, Chambers. It's my masterpiece. A beautiful death. I've recorded every second so everyone around the world can watch it as well. Once the media gets ahold of it, I'll be famous. Mackenzie will be famous. My beautiful death will be famous."

Staal finally stood up, holding a small pistol pointing straight at Dax.

Dax knew what was going to happen seconds before all hell broke loose. He screamed out, "Nooooooo, hold your fire!"

Just as the men around him opened fire on Jordan Charles Staal.

The smoke in the air was thick and choking. Dax coughed once, then twice as the air slowly cleared around them.

"Steady. Hold your positions!" Cruz yelled out. "Hold your fucking positions!"

Dax moved as if in a trance. He walked past the officers standing with their rifles now pointed at the ground, and around the side of the large desk Staal had been sitting behind. Dax felt as if he were having an out-of-body experience, he couldn't hear or see anything but Staal's dead body. He'd fallen backwards with the force of the bullets hitting his body, knocking the chair over in the process. He was lying on his back, arms outspread, blood slowly seeping into the light-blue carpet under Dax's feet. His legs were propped up on the seat of the tipped-over chair and his eyes were open, staring straight up. The gun, which Dax could now see was a fucking water pistol, lay next to his open hand, mockingly.

Dax moved his eyes to the desk top, turned the monitor Staal had twisted to face the doorway back to its original position, and groaned. He leaned over and propped himself on the desk with both hands and stared, not believing what he was seeing. The song coming through the speakers changed to the upbeat tones of the B-52s singing "Love Shack". The song so incongruent to what he was seeing, Dax could barely process it all.

There were three views of Mackenzie in the coffin. One was a viewpoint from the top corner of the small box. Another monitor showed a view from Mack's feet upward. Dax could see how small the box really was. Her breasts were almost brushing the top of the box and he could see her shift restlessly.

But it was the third view, on the monitor that Staal had turned to the room, that hit Dax the hardest. It was a close-up of Mack's face. It looked as though Staal had used a wide-angle lens and mounted it in the lid of the coffin, over her head.

Her eyes were huge, open wide as she struggled

to see something, anything. Her pupils were dilated as far as they could go. Dax could even see the tear tracks on her face from where she'd sobbed in fear. She had a dark spot on her forehead, where a bruise from hitting the lid of her tomb was forming. She was holding the satellite phone up to her ear with a death grip. He could see her struggling to breathe. Her mouth was open as if she was gasping for air, and not getting any. Every now and then she'd tilt her head back, as if doing so would mean what little air was left in her tomb could get into her lungs more easily.

Dax could hear some of the SRT members walking through the house, making sure there was no one else lurking around waiting to ambush them and that Staal really was working alone. A door opened, footsteps sounded on the floor above them, the low murmurings of the officers clearing the rooms as they searched. Dax figured it was useless. Staal wouldn't have Mack stashed here. He'd already buried her somewhere, he was sure of it.

TJ came up beside Dax and put his hand on his shoulder. "Fucking hell, Dax. Come on, you don't need to watch that."

Dax shrugged off TJ's touch violently. "Don't touch me!"

"Let the guys get into the hard drives to see what they can get. There's still time to find her, Dax."

Dax just shook his head. "It's too late. Look, TJ." He turned to his friend, throwing out a hand. "Fucking *look*! Without Staal here to tell us where she is, it's too late. We'll take too long. We'll never find her in time." Dax said the words, but readily moved when two officers came up behind him. One immediately started typing, careful not to blacken the screen with Mackenzie's face on it, knowing Dax would lose it if he lost sight of her.

"Maybe we can track the feed," one of the officers said to the other, entirely focused on what he was doing.

"Yeah, see if you can pinpoint where it starts. If it's within a few miles we can be there in minutes."

Ignoring the two men frantically trying to use their computer knowledge to find out where Staal had stashed Mackenzie, Dax ran his finger over the screen as if he was actually touching Mack's cheek. "God." The word was spoken with such angst, it was obvious to everyone in the room Dax was suffering.

TJ had no words for his friend, and finally backed off, leaving Dax to his grief.

"Dax, your phone." It was Quint. He'd run out to his patrol car and retrieved their phones. "The last words she hears should be yours."

Dax took the phones Quint held out with shaking fingers. There was still music coming from it. Mack was still hearing the sound of cheesy eighties melodies in her coffin. Dax didn't know if he could do it. He looked back at the monitor.

He didn't have a choice. For Mack. She should hear his voice, the voice of the man she loved, and who loved her back with his entire being.

He tapped off the music on Quint's phone and brought his own phone up to his ear.

"Hey, sweetheart. I'm back." Dax's voice was low and soothing and eerily echoed out of the speakers on the desktop.

"Daxton."

Dax took a deep breath. He loved hearing his name come from her mouth. He watched as Mackenzie shut her eyes and opened her mouth wider, trying to get air that wasn't available into her lungs.

"Please be quiet and listen, Mack. Relax. Close your eyes and let it happen. I'm right here with you. I have a story for you. This is a story of a boy who dreamed of a girl made just for him. This boy had the same dream every night. Every single night of his life, he dreamed of a special woman. Not a princess, not a millionaire, but a plain ol' hardworking woman. As the years went by, and he grew older, he continued to have the dream. He lived his life, made friends, dated, but not one woman he met was the one of his dreams. He dreamed about how she wasn't perfect. She made mistakes, but owned up to them immediately. She was clumsy and silly and had a tendency to pratter on when she was telling a story or when she was nervous. The man wanted that dream woman more than he could say, but she never appeared."

Dax cleared his throat, and tried to control the tears gathering in his throat and his eyes. He watched as a tear came out the side of Mack's eye as she lay gasping for breath and he dug deep to find the strength to continue. To give her this. Her last moments should be filled with the sound of his voice, not the sound of silence or some fucking pop song from years ago.

"One day the man met a woman, he said hello politely and went on his way, not knowing he'd just met the woman he'd dreamed about his entire life. Luckily, fate had pity on the couple, as they met again not long after. One day led to the next and before he knew what hit him, the man realized he hadn't dreamed of his special dream woman in weeks. He mourned the loss, until he realized there was no need to dream about her anymore, she was standing right in front of him.

"Mack, sweetheart. You're that woman. I've dreamed of you my entire life. I might not have had you for long, but I'll treasure every second you were in my arms, my bed and in my life. I love you, Mackenzie Morgan. You will not be forgotten. Not by me. Not by your family, not by any-fucking-body. Relax now, baby. Stop fighting. It's okay. I'm here with you now."

Dax watched through the tears in his eyes as Mackenzie's hand went lax and the phone she'd been holding fell by her head. Her mouth stopped gaping open and shut and she lay still, her eyes staring up at the camera, not blinking.

Dax clicked his phone off and put his hand on Mack's face on the monitor. She was gone.

A single tear coursed down Dax's cheek and he felt hollow inside. "I love you, Mack. There'll never be another like you."

CHAPTER 17

"Dax! Move your ass!" Cruz's words were sharp and urgent and came from somewhere in the house.

Dax could tell his friend was shouting the words, as he heard them come from another room, but they also seemed to be coming from the speakers on the desk in front of him. Dax looked at the officers working on the computer next to him, they gazed back at him, eyes wide with disbelief.

Dax didn't want to go anywhere. He didn't care that Staal's dead body was on the floor behind him. He didn't care about anything but staying right where he was, being with Mackenzie. He didn't know how he'd get through the rest of the night, or the following day, or the next. He had a million things to do. He had to get ahold of Mackenzie's family and Laine. He had to... Hell, he had no idea *what* he needed to do.

"Seriously, Dax. Get your ass down here. Right fucking now!"

The words, louder in the room now that the officer next to him had turned up the volume on the speaker, made Dax stand up abruptly. Now that he was beginning to be able to think again he knew there was only one reason he'd be hearing his friend through the speakers of the computer Staal had been sitting in front of.

"Where the hell are you?" Dax roared, already on the move.

"Basement. Now, Dax!"

Dax jogged through a room with a sofa and TV to an open door, following the pointing finger of the officer standing next to it. Obviously while he was saying good-bye to Mack, Cruz had been searching the house with the other officers. On auto-pilot, Dax pulled out his weapon and moved down the stairs, having a feeling he knew what he'd find.

Dax stopped dead in his tracks at the bottom of the stairs.

In the middle of the room was a large wooden rectangular box. It was sitting on a pedestal and there were four wires leading from the box up into the ceiling. He had a hard time processing what he was seeing. Dax's mind was still up in the office with Mackenzie.

Dax met Cruz's eyes.

"Look around, grab anything you can to help me get the lid off. It's nailed shut with about a million nails. We need something to help us get in there." Cruz's words were frantic as he and two other officers did their best to force the lid up by brute strength alone, with no luck.

Dax shoved his pistol into the holster at his back and looked around quickly, realizing what the hell was going on. His heart beat fast in his chest. How long had it been since he'd seen Mack take her last breath? If he was lucky, she might still have a chance. Dax spied a metal pipe leaning against a wall and grabbed it. He shoved it into Cruz's hands, hoping it would work. Dax continued to scan the room to see what else he could find.

There! A crowbar. Exactly what he needed.

Dax grabbed it and rushed over to Cruz's side. He put the end under the lid and pushed. At first he didn't think it was going to move, but finally Dax felt the lid move a tiny bit. With one more heave, getting help from Cruz and the others around the coffin and putting pressure on the metal tool, the lid finally shifted an inch.

"Grab it. Get it off!" Cruz's words were barked to the other officers. Every man around the box forced their fingers under the rim of the make-shift coffin, and pulled with all their might.

Dax held his breath as the lid was pushed open.

Mack.

She lay still, not moving, not breathing. She looked exactly like she did on the damn monitor. Her eyes were open, staring sightlessly up, her mouth parted, her hand lying lifeless next to her head. At her feet were piles of dirt. Staal had obviously dumped it into the coffin, ensuring she'd smell it and believe she was actually underground. Fucking bastard.

Dax didn't hesitate, but leaned over and scooped Mack up into his arms and lifted her from the damn tomb she'd been ensconced in and immediately laid her on the floor.

"Call the paramedics," he ordered Cruz.

"Already on their way, Ranger," one of the other officers said quickly.

Dax turned back to Mackenzie. He couldn't lose her now. Not when he'd been so close. She'd held on for too long for two damn minutes to make a difference between tearing his heart out or making his life complete.

Dax put two fingers on Mack's neck and felt a

faint pulse. "She's got a heartbeat," he announced to no one in particular. She wasn't breathing though. He needed to get air into her lungs. He tilted her head back. Dax put one hand on her bruised forehead and the other on her chin, pulling her lip down. He leaned over and breathed twice into her mouth, pushing much-needed oxygen into her lungs.

"Come on, Mack. Come on, baby."

He breathed into her again.

"You can do it. Come on. Don't let him win."

He leaned over and breathed into Mack's mouth again.

"Come back to me, sweetheart. I need you."

Dax did it again, then again.

He firmed his voice. "Breathe, Mack. Fucking breathe already!"

Finally, Mackenzie coughed once, low, and Dax held his breath. "That's it, Mack. You can do it. Breathe, baby."

Dax wanted nothing more than to take Mack into his arms, but knew it wouldn't be smart. He kept his hands on her head and kept encouraging her. She slowly coughed harder and harder and finally Dax could see her gulping in air on her own.

He leaned down into her. "I'm so proud of you. You did it. Thank God. Thank you, Jesus." Dax sobbed into Mack's hair until the paramedics arrived.

* * *

DAX HELD MACKENZIE'S HAND, refusing to let go, all the way to the hospital. Cruz brushed aside his thanks, telling him to "go with your woman." Dax didn't have to be told twice.

Mackenzie hadn't fully woken up yet. She had regained consciousness twice, but was obviously still confused about where she was and what had happened. She had an IV inserted and was being given oxygen. Dax hadn't seen any wounds on her, other than the bruise on her forehead, but wasn't taking any chances.

He'd refused to leave her room, telling the doctors she was under the Texas Rangers' protection, which wasn't exactly a lie. The nurses had changed her out of her soiled clothes and put her into a gown. After the doctor had examined her, they'd stuffed her under the covers, and Dax was finally alone with her.

He sat down next to the hospital bed and picked up Mack's hand. Her nails had been ripped and broken in her initial struggles when she'd awoken in the coffin and tried unsuccessfully to claw her way out, but otherwise she looked fine. Dax kissed each finger gently and rested his head on top of her hand on the mattress.

Now that the adrenaline was wearing off, and he knew Mack was safe and unharmed, Dax was exhausted. He quickly fell asleep, with one hand clasping Mack's and the other laying possessively and reassuringly on her stomach.

Mackenzie woke slowly and shifted, feeling something heavy on her belly. Suddenly remembering everything, she opened her eyes, then closed them immediately against the harsh light in the room.

Light. That's all she needed to know.

She wasn't buried alive anymore. Dax had found her, gotten to her.

She knew she'd had a close call. She recalled every second of straining to breathe, and not being able to get any oxygen into her lungs. She had no idea what had happened and how she'd been rescued, she just thanked God Daxton had done it.

Mackenzie moved a hand to her stomach and covered the hand that was laying there. Daxton's. She'd know it anywhere.

Mackenzie turned and squinted her eyes open this time, being more cautious now that she knew she was safe and with Daxton. All she could see was his hair. He was sound asleep, trapping her left hand under his head. Mack closed her eyes again.

Safe and with Daxton, that was all she needed to know. She fell asleep again without a further thought.

* * *

"So you're telling me I wasn't buried alive at all?"

Mackenzie was sitting with Cruz, Quint, TJ, Calder, Conor, Hayden, and Laine in Daxton's apartment. She'd been released from the hospital a few hours ago and all of Daxton's friends, and Laine, had come over to see how she was doing.

"Nope. Fucker didn't actually bury anyone until after they'd died."

"Seriously? Man, that is fucked up."

Everyone laughed, even though it really wasn't funny.

"He'd run cameras into the coffin and was upstairs watching you. He was also listening to your phone call to Dax, getting off on it." Cruz laid it out for Mackenzie. He'd had a talk, privately, with Dax and asked what he thought Mackenzie should know. Dax had told him to say what he wanted, but if Dax thought Mack wasn't dealing, then he'd cut it off. So far, Mack was dealing just fine. She was amazing.

"I mean, really? It's one thing to kidnap women. It's another to want them for sexual shit. But he didn't even touch me. He didn't hurt me in any way. For him, it was all psychological torture? What a sick, sick man." Mackenzie held on to Daxton's hand tightly. It was hard to believe she'd made it through what she had, but she refused to dwell on it. She wouldn't give the Lone Star Reaper that.

"Apparently his mom taught him all he needed to know about killing when he was a young child. She made him watch as she suffocated his little brother, helped kidnap a little girl in the neighborhood, and they killed her the same way he ended up killing all those other women. But karma always wins; she taught him so well, Staal ended up killing his own mother, and then couldn't stop. We figure he killed his wife, but I'm not sure her body will ever be found. If he buried her coffin somewhere, it's probably better she's allowed to rest in peace. Somehow along the way, he fixated on law enforcement, specifically Dax here, and the rest is history."

Mackenzie turned to Daxton. "He was filming me in there?"

"Yeah, baby. He was."

"Are the tapes...will others see them?"

Dax turned to Mack and put his hands on her face. "Look at me, Mack. No one will see those tapes.

I swear to you. Cruz took them. They're at the FBI. They won't go anywhere."

"I—"

"You're safe. The things you said to me. The stuff I said back. They're between us. No one else gets that. It's ours. Okay?"

"Okay. I get it. But, Daxton. If someone can learn from what he did, from what's on those tapes, I think we should let them see them. I don't remember some of the stuff I said, and I'm sure I was a big dork, but if somehow the FBI or whoever can use something to prevent this from happening again, I'm okay with that. Or maybe doctors somewhere can use them to see what happens during asphyxiation. Calder, do you think the medical examiner's office could use them?"

Dax pulled Mack into his arms. "Don't answer that, Calder. My Mack. Always thinking about others, aren't you?"

"Well, I'm not doing cartwheels that my last breaths—well, my almost-last breaths—are on tape in some deep dark vault somewhere, and I certainly never want to see it, and I don't want *you* to have to see that again, but Daxton, I'd feel bad to ask to have them destroyed if some good could come out of them."

"I love you, Mackenzie Morgan."

"And I love you, Daxton Chambers, but you *are* hearing what I'm saying, aren't you?"

"I hear you, baby. But trust me when I say, you taking your last breaths of oxygen, is not something anyone else can ever learn from."

Mackenzie snuggled into Daxton's arms, ignoring the others around them. "I hate him."

"Me too."

"But I hate him for what he did to *you* more than what he did to me. It's one thing to know, abstractly, that I'm dying, it's another thing altogether to see someone you love dying. I hate that he did that to you. I wish I could make you unsee it."

"Mack—"

"No, really. It's like when I was thirteen and I accidentally walked into the bathroom when Matthew was in there. I can never unsee that. Seriously. Seeing your brother's you-know-what when you're on the verge of womanhood is never a good thing. I thought I'd be scarred for life. I'm surprised I even let Donny what's-his-name get to second base at prom when I was a junior. All I'm saying is that some things can't be unseen, and that's one of those things that should never have been seen in the first place. Damn Jordan whatever, for doing that to you. It sucks, and I hate it. I'm glad he's dead. I'm glad he got blown away. Fucker."

"Bloodthirsty little thing, isn't she?" Conor commented from the chair across from the sofa.

"Yeah." Dax's agreement was soft and heartfelt. "All I see now is you, here in my arms. Alive, breathing, and making me want to laugh and roll my eyes at the same time, Mack. Go with it."

"Okay. Are you guys hungry? I'm hungry. They wouldn't give me anything at the hospital and Daxton wouldn't stop to get me fries on the way home. Anyone want pizza? Maybe we can order some pizza. Oh and Daxton, you heard Mark and Matthew are coming over right? We never did get to that family get-together we had planned. Between your job and me being kidnapped by a psycho serial killer, we haven't made it over there yet. There was no way I could say no when they said they wanted to see me. Don't be surprised if mom comes over with them."

"I knew they were coming, Mack. No worries."

"Okay, but remember what I said about them. They're a little crazy."

Laine piped in at that. "They *are* a little crazy. Mack, remember that time we wanted to go to that party and Matthew busted us? I said I'd be at your house and you said you'd be at mine. He came home from college and wanted to see you and called over to my house. My mom told him we were at *your* house. He knew where the party was usually held, and pulled us out of that hotel room kicking and screaming.

Mackenzie smiled at her friend. "Yeah, how embarrassing." She looked back at Daxton. "See? Even my best friend thinks my family is crazy."

"Okay, sweetheart."

"Good. Oh, and are we still going to Austin? Because I think I could go for that. Hotel Ella sounded so awesome. I looked it up and did you know some of the suites are bigger than my apartment? Don't get one of those, though, what a waste of space, especially if we're going to spend all our time in bed. Oh shit, I didn't mean to say that out loud. Please forget you heard that, guys. Oh, and you should know, I'm not a Longhorn fan. I know, it's sacriligious, but I thought you should know in case you wanted to walk around the UT campus oohing and ahhing about everything. I'm weird and couldn't really give a crap about football or basketball or anything related to college. I went, got my degree, and I'm really proud of that, but I'm not into all the hoopla with the sports. Sorry."

"It's okay, Mack."

"But I *am* a fan of law enforcement. I've always loved a man in uniform and I think I love them even more now that my rescue went down with like four different agencies participating. It's a girl's dream come true, no offense, Hayden. You're hot in your uniform too, though I don't go that way, but it's okay if you—"

Dax had enough. He leaned over, cutting off Mack's passionate babbling with a gentle hand on her mouth. "You mean, *I'm* your dream come true."

Mackenzie turned her serious eyes up to Daxton. When he moved his hand she said, "I vaguely remember you telling me a story about a little boy dreaming about the girl of his dreams. Didn't I?" At Daxton's nod, she continued. "I had the same dream. I knew I'd find you, it just took longer than I wanted it to."

"I love you, Mack."

"I love you back, Daxton."

"Enough snutaling on the couch, you two. Mack's family is coming over, you better not be naked when they get here," TJ warned with a laugh.

"Snutaling? Is that a word?" Mackenzie asked chuckling.

"Who cares? You get what I mean."

"Okay, Daxton will stop snutaling. I need to get up and get ready to see my family."

Dax kissed Mack on the lips hard. "You look fine the way you are, Cruz will get the door when they get here."

Without a word of protest, Mackenzie eased herself back into Daxton's arms. If she didn't have to get up, she wouldn't. There was no place she'd rather be than right there, safe, in Daxton's arms, surrounded by their friends.

CHAPTER 18

MACKENZIE STRETCHED, feeling delicious. She felt a hand on her stomach and then felt Daxton lick at her folds. She groaned in delight. "Oh my God, Daxton. Seriously?"

"I can't get enough of you…of us."

"Aren't you tired? What time is it?"

Dax grinned up at Mackenzie. He'd left the table lamp on next to the bed so he could see Mack as he made love with her. "It's around three."

"Daxton," Mackenzie moaned and squirmed in his grip as he ran his hands over her stomach and down to her thighs, parting them so he could fit more comfortably between them. "It's only been two hours since you last made love to me. You can't possibly be ready to go again."

"Mack, I'm not fifteen anymore, of course I'm not

ready to go again yet, but I can't resist you. And women aren't made like men are. You can come over and over."

"Daxton…" The word came out as a whine.

"This time we're coming together, sweetheart. No, don't protest. I haven't pushed, and you're so primed, you'll be screaming my name before too long. It'll take me longer to get there so we'll have time to work you up, this won't be a problem. Trust me."

"Touch me, Daxton. Please. I need you."

Dax pushed one finger into Mackenzie's folds and felt her clench down on him. "This is just as sexy as I knew it would be. You are fucking soaked with both our juices. I wish you could see yourself. My cum is slowly seeping out of you, and the more worked up you get, the faster it comes out." Dax knew he was being crude, but he couldn't help it. He scooped up some of their juices with his fingers and brought it to his mouth. "Fucking fantastic."

Before Mack could say anything, Dax moved so he was on his back and Mackenzie was straddling his stomach. He held on to her hips with his hands until she was steady.

Mackenzie looked down at Daxton with heavy-lidded eyes, ready for whatever he wanted. They'd been adventurous in bed, and if he wanted her to ride him, she was ready. They'd done that before and he'd made her explode right before he'd taken her hard.

"Come up here, I want more of that."

"Oh my God, Daxton, no."

Ignoring her embarrassment, Dax grabbed Mack by her hips and encouraged her to scoot up his chest until she was kneeling over him. He looked up at her folds before moving. "Yes. Can you feel us, Mack?"

She could. Mack could feel their fluids dripping from inside her to dampen her inner thighs. "Daxton…" She tried again to move.

"Oh no, stay right where you are." Dax pulled Mack down to him and got to work building her up to another orgasm. He used his lips and his mouth to lick and suck until she was shaking and he knew she was on the verge of exploding.

Mackenzie had never, in all her sexually active years, had a man want to taste her after he'd come inside her. She thought it'd be weird, or even gross, but if she was honest with herself, it was hotter than hell.

Dax pushed Mack down his body, loving the feel of her wetness smearing over his chest and stomach. Finally she rested on his lower abs. "Take me in your hand, baby. Feel how much I love this, love you. Put me in. Take me."

He didn't have to say it twice. Mackenzie rose on her knees just far enough to reach under herself and grab him. She fit him to her, scooted back into place and sank down with a groan.

"That's it. Now ride me, Mack. Take what you need. Take me."

Mackenzie concentrated on the amazing feeling of Dax inside her. She could feel him flex within her and she squeezed him as she pulled up, then slammed back down. She placed her hands on his chest to brace herself, and did it again, then again. Each time she came down on him, she clasped him with her inner muscles with all her strength.

Dax reached up, took Mack's breasts in his hands, and grasped her a little harder than he would if they were just getting started. He pinched her nipples. "Harder, Mack. Do it. Fuck me, baby."

At his words, Mackenzie did as he asked. She slammed herself up and down on Dax, lost in the exquisite sensations.

"Touch yourself, Mack. Rub your clit. Do it. Now. Make yourself come all over my dick."

Lost in the moment, and not feeling any embarrassment, Mackenzie trailed one hand where they were joined and rubbed against her bundle of nerves, hard. She immediately felt the orgasm building.

"It's coming, Daxton. Almost…"

"Keep riding me, baby. There you go. You're beautiful. Fucking beautiful, and mine. Keep going, harder. That's it."

Mackenzie let Daxton's words wash over her. She *felt* beautiful. In his arms, in his bed, she felt like the prettiest woman in the world. She wasn't thinking about what had happened to her with Staal or of how awkward sex had been previously for her. Her orgasm was coming, and coming fast.

She touched herself one last time and hunched forward as she felt her orgasm start to move through her. "Oh God, yes, Daxton!"

Dax felt the fingernails of Mack's left hand digging into his chest and ignored them. He slammed Mack down on himself twice more then held her there as she shook and trembled in his arms through her climax.

Finally, he eased her down, still twitching. "Easy, Mack. That's it. Just relax. I've got you. Good girl." Dax continued to murmur to her until she finally came back to herself and her surroundings.

"You killed me, Daxton. Seriously. But you didn't—"

"I did."

"What?"

Dax chuckled. "We came at the same time,

sweetheart."

Mackenzie sat up and braced herself on Daxton's chest. "No we didn't."

"Yeah, we did." Dax rubbed one thumb over Mack's sensitive clit and she shuddered. "Can't you feel me inside? You drained me dry, Mack. We came together."

Mackenzie burst into tears and collapsed on his chest. Dax simply wrapped his arms around the woman he loved and smiled, waiting for her to get it all out, knowing why she was crying.

"I d-d-didn't think I'd ever be able to—"

"Shhhh, I know. I knew you could. You just needed to get out of your head to do it."

"I love you. I fucking love you so much."

"I love you too, Mack. And just so you know, that wasn't a one-off. It's gonna happen again. Not every time, no. But it will happen again."

"Good. I liked it."

"Good. Sleep, baby."

"Are you gonna let me sleep? Or are you gonna wake me up in twenty minutes to go again?"

Dax chuckled. "Sleep for now. We'll play it by ear and see how it goes."

Dax held Mackenzie close, still inside her, as she slid into sleep. He brushed her hair back behind her ear and listened to her breathe. He'd never take such a simple thing for granted again. Seeing Mack take her last breath would haunt him for the rest of his life. He was very grateful he'd been able to get to her in time to breathe life back into her, but it'd been close, too close.

Thank God for Cruz searching Staal's house so quickly after everything had gone down. If it hadn't been for him, they wouldn't have found Mack in time. If they'd found her twenty minutes, ten minutes...hell, even five minutes later than they did, he would've had to stand at the side of her grave in a cemetery. He owed Cruz everything.

Dax had driven to Austin with Mack to Hotel Ella to hide out after the press had hounded them. Everyone wanted an interview with the woman who'd been kidnapped by a serial killer, and died, but then been brought back to life. Mackenzie had given a few interviews then called it quits. She'd told Dax she understood why people were curious, and she'd told her story, but enough was enough.

They'd been in Austin for three days, and just like they'd originally planned, hadn't left the hotel room and hadn't worn any real clothes for the entire time they'd been there. They'd just enjoyed being with each other, alive and well.

Dax leaned down and kissed the top of Mack's head. He was the luckiest man in the world.

EPILOGUE

"I DON'T LIKE IT, CRUZ." Daxton tried to reason with his friend. "Why the hell do you have to be the one?"

"Look, it's only for a couple of months, then I'll be back. There simply isn't anyone else who can do it."

"Bullshit. Going undercover for months isn't healthy. I've known too many people who get completely fucked up in the head by being under for too long."

"I appreciate your concern, Dax, but I'm doing it."

Dax sighed and ran his hand through his hair. "Tell me again what you can."

"You know as well as I do the drug situation is getting out of control. We do everything possible, but they won't stop. I'm going undercover to try to see if I can find out where they're coming from. We keep getting the low-level players, and they don't matter. We need to find the source."

"And how do you think you'll be able to infiltrate the drug ring in a month or so without drawing suspicion to yourself?"

Cruz sighed, knowing his friend wasn't going to like what he had to tell him. "We think we know who the mid-level man of one of the drug rings is. He's the leader of a motorcycle gang. Word is that he has a girlfriend who doesn't know anything about what he's doing. I don't believe it. I'm going to see if I can—"

"Fuck, Cruz!" Dax exploded. "You can't bring a woman into this. You know as well as I do how fucked-up that is. Not to mention, cozying up to an MC president's girlfriend isn't the smartest move."

"Look, first, she's *already* in it, I'm not bringing her into anything. Innocent or not, whether she knows what's going on or not, she's in there. All I'm going to do is see if I can't get her to open up to me. I want to check it out, see if she's as innocent as the other agents think she is. Personally, I think she's hiding something. How the hell can she not know her boyfriend is a fucking drug runner? Do you know how many people have been killed by this shit?"

"You're using her." Dax knew how it worked.

He'd done an undercover assignment or two in his time, but he wasn't sure this one was a good idea.

"Yeah, but think of how many lives I'll be saving."

"You'll stay in touch?"

Cruz smiled at his friend. "Yeah, I'll stay in touch."

"If you need help, you'll let me know?"

"Yeah."

"You were there for me when Mack was taken. I'm not taking this lightly, Cruz. You're my brother, I'd do anything for you. Promise me, if this shit goes bad, you'll get out. You know how upset Mack would be if something happened to you. Hell, she's not going to like that she can't talk to you for a couple of months. You'd better find some way to appease her."

Cruz grinned. He loved how Mackenzie and Dax were together. Dax was a completely different person around Mack, and didn't give a fuck how cheesy he acted. They were in love. Truly in love. Cruz was happy for his friend.

"I will. Give her my love, will ya?"

"Yeah, and the others will want to know what's going on as well. If you just disappear for a couple of months, they're gonna notice and question it."

That was another thing that had come out of Mackenzie's kidnapping and Staal's death. The group of friends had gotten even closer. They made it a point now to hang out together. They went out for drinks, and had dinner together all the time. Even though they were all from different law enforcement agencies, with different priorities and missions, they were all on the same side. Working together to find and rescue Mackenzie had solidified their relationships.

"I thought maybe you could let them know what was up once I was gone."

"Fucking hell, Cruz."

"Well?"

"Okay, shit. Yeah, I'll let them know. Only if you check in regularly though."

"You got it."

"Keep your head down. Don't let them catch on. And don't fuck with that woman. If she knows, fine, get out and let your Director know. If she doesn't, do what you can to get her away from him, but if she won't go, fuck it. Don't get caught in the middle."

"This isn't my first rodeo, Dax. I fucking know how this works."

"Okay then. I'll talk to you soon, and see you in a few months?"

"Yeah."

"Stay safe, my friend."

"You too, Dax."

Cruz walked away, his mind already moving to his upcoming undercover mission. He'd take down the drug ring if it was the last thing he did. He didn't care who got in his way; he'd use his own mother, God rest her soul, if it meant getting more drugs off the street. He owed his ex-wife that, at the very least.

It wouldn't change anything for her, or them, but maybe it would for someone else.

* * *

LOOK for the next book in the Badge of Honor Series:

Justice for Mickie. Available now!

JOIN my Newsletter and find out about sales, free books, contests and new releases before anyone else!! Click HERE

Want to know when my books go on sale? Follow me on Bookbub HERE!

SCROLL to the end of this book to read the first chapter of Mickie and Cruz's story.

* * *

FOR CRUZ LIVINGSTON, becoming an FBI agent is a lifelong dream, guarding the streets of San Antonio a calling. His latest assignment—infiltrating the Red Brothers Motorcycle Club—will help stem the flow of illegal drugs brought into the city by the violent gang. He expects the job to be dangerous. He doesn't expect to meet the woman of his dreams while undercover.

Mickie Kaiser is refreshingly sweet, but her sister is intimately involved with the RBMC's president. Cruz can't afford to come clean about his double life without putting his operation in danger, but as violence creeps ever closer to Mickie, his priority becomes crystal clear. Cruz will do anything to keep Mickie alive...even if it means losing her love.

* *JUSTICE FOR MICKIE* is the 2nd book in the Badge of Honor: Texas Heroes series. Each book is a stand-alone, with no cliffhanger endings.

** This story features some very bad men, doing very bad things. The Red Brothers MC is up to its eyeballs in criminal and nefarious activities, including drugs, violence, and sexual abuse. The Brothers definitely don't know how to treat their women…but our alpha FBI hero does. And he's determined to protect *his* woman from the MC. At any cost.

To sign up for Susan's Newsletter go to: http://www.stokeraces.com/contact-1.html

Would you like Susan's Book Protecting Caroline for FREE?

Click HERE

Also by Susan Stoker

Badge of Honor: Texas Heroes Series

Justice for Mackenzie

Justice for Mickie

Justice for Corrie

Justice for Laine (novella)

Shelter for Elizabeth

Justice for Boone

Shelter for Adeline

Shelter for Sophie

Justice for Erin

Justice for Milena

Shelter for Blythe

Justice for Hope

Shelter for Quinn

Shelter for Koren

Shelter for Penelope

Delta Team Two Series

Shielding Gillian

Shielding Kinley (Aug 2020)

Shielding Aspen (Oct 2020)

Shielding Riley (Jan 2021)

Shielding Devyn (May 2021)

Shielding Ember (Sept 2021)

Shielding Sierra (TBA)

Delta Force Heroes Series
Rescuing Rayne
Rescuing Aimee (novella)
Rescuing Emily
Rescuing Harley
Marrying Emily (novella)
Rescuing Kassie
Rescuing Bryn
Rescuing Casey
Rescuing Sadie (novella)
Rescuing Wendy
Rescuing Mary
Rescuing Macie (novella)

SEAL of Protection: Legacy Series
Securing Caite
Securing Brenae (novella)
Securing Sidney
Securing Piper
Securing Zoey
Securing Avery (May 2020)
Securing Kalee (Sept 2020)
Securing Jane (novella) (Feb 2021)

SEAL Team Hawaii Series

Finding Elodie (Apr 2021)
Finding Lexie (Aug 2021)
Finding Kenna (Oct 2021)
Finding Monica (TBA)
Finding Carly (TBA)
Finding Ashlyn (TBA)

Ace Security Series

Claiming Grace
Claiming Alexis
Claiming Bailey
Claiming Felicity
Claiming Sarah

Mountain Mercenaries Series

Defending Allye
Defending Chloe
Defending Morgan
Defending Harlow
Defending Everly
Defending Zara
Defending Raven (June 2020)

Silverstone Series

Trusting Skylar (Dec 2020)
Trusting Taylor (Mar 2021)
Trusting Molly (July 2021)

Trusting Cassidy (Dec 2021

SEAL of Protection Series

Protecting Caroline

Protecting Alabama

Protecting Fiona

Marrying Caroline (novella)

Protecting Summer

Protecting Cheyenne

Protecting Jessyka

Protecting Julie (novella)

Protecting Melody

Protecting the Future

Protecting Kiera (novella)

Protecting Alabama's Kids (novella)

Protecting Dakota

Stand Alone

The Guardian Mist

Nature's Rift

A Princess for Cale

A Moment in Time- A Collection of Short Stories

Lambert's Lady

Special Operations Fan Fiction

http://www.AcesPress.com

Beyond Reality Series

Outback Hearts

Flaming Hearts

Frozen Hearts

Writing as Annie George:

Stepbrother Virgin (erotic novella)

ABOUT THE AUTHOR

New York Times, USA Today and *Wall Street Journal* Bestselling Author Susan Stoker has a heart as big as the state of Texas where she lives, but this all American girl has also spent the last fourteen years living in Missouri, California, Colorado, and Indiana. She's married to a retired Army man who now gets to follow *her* around the country.

She debuted her first series in 2014 and quickly followed that up with the SEAL of Protection Series, which solidified her love of writing and creating stories readers can get lost in.

If you enjoyed this book, or any book, please consider leaving a review. It's appreciated by authors more than you'll know.

www.stokeraces.com
susan@stokeraces.com

JUSTICE FOR MICKIE SAMPLE

For Cruz Livingston, becoming an FBI agent is a lifelong dream, guarding the streets of San Antonio a calling. His latest assignment—infiltrating the Red Brothers Motorcycle Club—will help stem the flow of illegal drugs brought into the city by the violent gang. He expects the job to be dangerous. He doesn't expect to meet the woman of his dreams while undercover.

Mickie Kaiser is refreshingly sweet, but her sister is intimately involved with the RBMC's president. Cruz can't afford to come clean about his double life without putting his operation in danger, but as violence creeps ever closer to Mickie, his priority becomes crystal clear. Cruz will do anything to keep Mickie alive…even if it means losing her love.

* *Justice for Mickie* is the 2nd book in the Badge of Honor: Texas Heroes series. Each book is a stand-alone, with no cliffhanger endings.

** This story features some very bad men, doing very bad things. The Red Brothers MC is up to its eyeballs in criminal and nefarious activities, including drugs, violence, and sexual abuse. The Brothers definitely don't know how to treat their women…but our alpha FBI hero does. And he's determined to protect *his* woman from the MC. At any cost.

CHAPTER 1

CRUZ LIVINGSTON TOOK a deep breath and willed himself to relax. He'd been undercover with the Red Brothers Motorcycle Club for a month—no, twenty-six days to be exact—and in his eyes, it was twenty-six days too long. Undercover assignments were never easy, but this had been like taking a fiery trip to hell the entire time.

He hadn't expected the job to be sunshine and roses, but he'd obviously gotten soft, because Cruz knew some of the shit he'd been forced to do to "prove" himself would haunt him for a long time. He hadn't killed or been pushed to rape anyone, thank God, but he'd threatened and beaten men up, and sold drugs. It was the selling of the drugs that had almost broken him.

It was ironic, the very reason he'd gone undercover—to *stop* the sale of drugs—was what he'd been forced to do from the very start of this assignment.

Cruz hadn't seen much of Ransom's supposed girlfriend, the person he was supposed to be getting close to in order to get information about the president. Her name was Angel, but from what Cruz could tell, she wasn't much of a girlfriend, more like a woman he was screwing. Cruz had seen Ransom fuck women in the middle of the clubhouse, not caring who was watching, so he obviously wasn't concerned about being exclusive with Angel.

Cruz's original plan had been to get in tight with the girlfriend and see what he could find out about the operation through her. But he had quickly found out that wasn't going to work. Ransom didn't give a shit about Angel, so it would look extremely odd for him to be cozying up to the woman.

MCs typically had two types of women hanging around—bikers' old ladies and club whores. The old ladies were somewhat respected by the other members of the club, and weren't ever disrespected by the whores or anyone outside the tight-knit group. The whores, on the other hand, were there to fuck and to use. Period. The whores knew their place, and never complained about it, ever hopeful that one day they might catch the eye of one of the members and become an old lady.

Cruz figured many of them continued to hang around for the drugs they were given in return for their services far more than they wanted to be an old lady. It was hard for him to fathom why any woman would allow herself to be mistreated as the whores in this club were, free drugs or not.

In the twenty-six days Cruz had been a prospect of the club, he'd seen some of the worst treatment of women he'd ever had the misfortune to observe in all his life, and that was saying something. His job as a member of the FBI included some pretty gnarly things, but watching as a drugged-out, half-conscious woman got gang-banged by ten members of the Hermanos Rojos motorcycle club, who didn't give a shit how rough they were, was one of the worst. The only reason Cruz hadn't had to participate was because of his prospect status. Until he was deemed "worthy" of the club, he wasn't allowed to participate in the orgies. Thank God.

Cruz knew he couldn't save everyone, but watching the women essentially get raped by the MC members brought to mind his ex-wife. She'd never been raped, but Cruz hadn't been able to save her from other seedy parts of life.

Cruz shook his head, trying to get back into the game. Standing in the middle of the Red Brothers' clubhouse wasn't the time to remember his fucked up relationship with his ex-wife.

"Yo, Smoke, get your ass over here!" Ransom called from across the room.

Cruz had chosen the nickname Smoke when he'd joined the club. He hadn't bothered to explain it, letting the club members think what they wanted about the name. In actuality, it was his friend Dax who'd come up with the moniker. They'd joked that he was sneaky like smoke...getting into every crevice of the Hermanos Rojos's business and hopefully being the reason they were eventually taken down.

The only reason Cruz was able to infiltrate the MC was because an FBI agent who'd had a long-term undercover assignment at another club, near the border of Texas and Mexico, had vouched for Cruz when Ransom and his vice president had inquired. Simply being allowed in the clubhouse, and being privy to much of what went on there, was a huge step in being able to gather information on the club and hopefully stop one of the many entry points for drugs into the city.

He'd told Ransom and the others he was a part-time mall security cop. He had to have some sort of job, and doing anything directly related to law enforcement was definitely out, but he also needed a reason to look relatively clean-cut and not quite so "bikerish."

Cruz ambled over to where Kitty, Tick, and three other members of the club were standing.

"What's up?" Cruz asked with a chin lift to the guys.

"Got a job for ya," Ransom said with disdain, obviously annoyed at something. "I'm keeping some pussy on the side, but she's getting to be a pain in my ass. You know, demanding and shit, but I've got plans for her, so I can't piss her off. She called and demanded to come over to the clubhouse tonight. I don't particularly like her ass anywhere near here, but if I want to get in there and use her to get more high-class customers, I have to give in. I need you to go and pick her ass up."

Cruz's mind spun. He figured Ransom was talking about Angel, but he hadn't been privy to what customers Ransom thought he could get by using her. Cruz wondered just what other plans the president of the club had.

"Sure thing. What's the bitch look like?" Cruz's words were sneered with just the right amount of attitude.

"She's tall and skinny with big tits, which makes her nice to fuck. She's got long blonde hair and fancies herself in love with a real live MC president."

The other guys laughed as if Ransom had said the funniest thing they'd ever heard.

"What's the draw, Pres?" Cruz knew he was pushing his luck, but he wanted to see if he could dig a bit deeper and see if getting in with Angel's friends was the only reason the man was hanging around her.

"The draw is that we're trying to expand business, and Angel is beautiful to look at but dumb as a rock. She's got access to a whole new set of customers...fancy-ass rich women, and we need to draw them in. She's so enamored of my role, and my cock, she'll do whatever I tell her to. I know she wants to continue to suck my MC president dick, so she'll do what I want, no questions asked."

Cruz didn't like what he was hearing, but kept his voice even. "So, I pick her ass up and bring her back here, then what?"

"Then we throw a lame-ass party with the old ladies, no whores around, she sees we're harmless, like a real-live, fucking romance novel or like that stupid-ass TV show, and she goes on her merry way. I get her hooked on me and the lifestyle she wants to believe in, as well as the drugs, and she'll be my ticket to selling to her rich friends."

Cruz's stomach turned. He wondered if this was how his ex had started out. He didn't know Angel, but there was no way he wanted to be a party to anything Ransom had in store for her, never mind her friends.

When he'd volunteered for the assignment, the goal was for him to gain some knowledge the FBI could use to remove just one of the avenues for drugs getting into the city, and if necessary, plant the seed for placing a more long-term agent inside the club. Since Cruz wasn't supposed to be there for months, he was to gather evidence about their drug-dealing so the agency could keep their eye on the club and, if things went as planned, bring down some of their contacts as well. No one knew how deep the Hermanos Rojos were with the big players.

Ransom wanting to use innocent women—although always a possibility; they'd known about Angel going in—was something that would never be all right with Cruz. If he could save Angel in the process of shutting down some of their supply lines before he got out, all the better.

"Sounds easy enough. Pick her up, bring her here. Got it. You got her address?"

"Better. I'm tracking her. Planted a bug in her purse. Bitch doesn't go anywhere without that huge-ass bag." Ransom flicked a small electronic device in Cruz's direction. "You'll see where she is. Bring her ass back here at eight. Not a second before. We'll do the party thing, I'll take her home, fuck her, and be back here by eleven. Then we can *really* party."

The other men around him laughed crudely.

Ransom focused on the other members of his club. "Make sure the whores are back by then. I'm in the mood for a gang bang tonight. Angel's tight pussy just won't be enough. There's nothing like fucking a whore when she's tied down and squirming for more."

Cruz laughed along with the other men at the president's words, while cringing inside.

"One more thing, Smoke," Ransom warned as Cruz started to leave.

Cruz turned back to the president and lifted his chin.

"Angel has a bitch of a sister who doesn't want her to have anything to do with the club. She's been riding Angel's ass, and I'm sick of it. Do whatever it takes to keep her skanky ass away, even if that means you put her out of commission for a while. That bitch had better not fuck with my plans, otherwise she'll find herself hurt in a way so she won't be *able* to mess with me."

Made in the USA
Monee, IL
18 July 2020

36701036R50164